
LOST LOVE FOUND

KAY LYONS

Kindred Spirits Publishing

Chapter 1

Holland Cohen walked to the stone railing of the private residence situated along the Intercoastal Waterway in Wilmington, North Carolina, and sighed.

"Beautiful, isn't it?"

Holland turned and saw an elegantly coiffed elderly woman smiling at her as she approached, an equally elegant cane in hand. Holland tried to pinpoint the woman's age but couldn't quite place her. Early to mid-eighties?

"I'm ninety-four, my dear." The woman's bright blue eyes sparkled with amusement. "If that's what's making you frown so."

Holland quickly schooled her features, an embarrassed laugh leaving her. "Hello, Mrs. Bane. I'm so glad you called me about donating to the charity auction."

"My friend Margaret speaks highly of you and your company. After meeting you at the ladies' luncheon, I knew I wanted to help. Would you like to talk out here or inside?"

Considering it was the first of March in North

Carolina and the temperature had reached a gloriously balmy seventy today, Holland wanted to stay outside and enjoy it while it lasted. North Carolina spring weather was decidedly mercurial, with warm temps one day and drastic, shiver-inducing drops the next. "Wherever you're most comfortable."

"It's a beautiful day. Let's sit here until it gets too chilly," the woman said, seating herself on one of the beautiful couches along the second-floor patio of the palatial home. "Margaret told me she's known you for a while. She said you handled the sale of some of her jewelry several years ago."

Holland waited until the woman was comfortably settled before lowering herself onto the settee opposite her. Only then did she remove the donation form from her bag. "I'm sorry, but I'm not at liberty to say much due to confidentiality clauses with my company, Mrs. Bane."

"Please, call me Violet."

"Violet," Holland said. "That said, I will say the company I work for is one of the best for the resale of high-end items if you ever find yourself wanting to redecorate." Handling the sale of a client's personal items had to be done with the utmost delicacy. So many people chose to use her company as a way of avoiding the public notice of selling items to recoup as much of the original cost as possible due to unspoken financial strain. But in the case of Violet Bane, Holland didn't think that was the case.

Was she here simply to confirm a donation for the upcoming auction, or did Violet have something else in mind?

She'd recognized the name immediately, but according to Holland's quick internet research, the Bane family was old-money, the kind that had survived the depression and thrived soon after. Industrial-era businesses, political posts, and well-to-do marriages had left the family name akin to that of the Kennedys and an American version of royalty.

"Tell me about yourself."

Holland blinked at the request. "Pardon?"

"My dear, the item is yours for the auction, have no fear. But I'd like to know more. Your bio said you're from the area?"

It appeared Violet Bane had also done her homework. "Uh, yes, ma'am. When I'm not traveling for work, I live in Carolina Cove."

"So you're from the Wilmington area originally? Are you married? Have a family?"

The housekeeper who had shown her to the balcony appeared carrying a tray with tea, cookies, and little pieces of scrumptious-looking cake sliced in generous proportions.

"Thank you, Sally."

Holland eyed the goodies and thought of the extra time she'd need in the gym just to cover this meeting alone. Not to mention the luncheon she'd had with another potential donor an hour or so earlier while in Southport.

"Ma'am? What would you like?" Sally asked.

"Oh, uh, a cookie, please." It seemed to be the less caloric of the choices but that cake… Why was she ruled by her sweet tooth?

"Go on, dear. You were saying?"

Holland accepted the plated cookie and met Violet's gaze, wondering if the source of the woman's questions was loneliness or simply shrewd business acumen. "I was born in Germany at a military hospital, and my parents settled us here after my father retired. He and my mother now own the Carolina Cove Pier and Inn."

"How nice. Places like that are such a boon for our economy and a lure for tourists to return to whenever a storm comes through and damages cause a downturn. What does your husband do?"

"I'm not married. Never have been."

"I find it hard to believe a woman as beautiful as you hasn't been asked."

Holland inhaled and struggled to keep a pleasant expression pinned to her face. "I have been. Once."

"Oh? What happened?"

Violet must have sensed she was going beyond the proper limits for two people who'd only met briefly two days ago, but her gaze remained direct, holding Holland's without flinching. "I… He was killed. He was a Special Forces soldier."

"Oh, my dear. I'm terribly sorry. It was recent?"

Holland shook her head, wondering how an appointment to pick up an auction item had turned into this. She cleared the lump from her throat and focused on the task at hand. "It was five years ago."

"The grieving doesn't go away, does it? Not when we truly love."

"Mmm," she said, avoiding the truth by simply agreeing. Her guilt came from turning down the proposal, knowing she didn't love David as much as a would-be wife should love a husband. He'd gone back to war, brokenhearted, and she would always wonder if she wasn't somehow to blame for his death since it had occurred so soon after. "The, um, item you wanted to donate… May I see it? I'll need to get some photos so I can begin the details page for the auction booklet."

"Soon, dear. Do you have children? Siblings?"

Southern. How could she forget that questions some might think of as intrusive really were just a southerner's way of getting to know someone? Personal questions were a handshake in the south. Just a nice-to-meet-you. "No children. I do have four sisters, though. One older and three younger. All them involved, engaged, or married with a baby on the way."

"How fun. Your parents must be thrilled."

"We all are."

"I had a sister. She died of polio when she was young."

"I'm sorry."

"As am I. I've often wondered what it would've been like to have been one of a houseful."

"Well, with all girls, plus my mother, my father found himself using the outdoor shower a lot, I can tell you that."

The older woman laughed at the comment and nodded several times.

"Yes, yes, I can see how that would have been difficult for him. Your name… Holland is a beautiful name, though unusual. Does it have special meaning?"

Holland settled back against the cushioned seat, leaving the contract for later, when Violet Bane finally satisfied her curiosity after her game of Twenty Questions. "Military family," she said again simply. "My parents named us after where we were conceived."

The woman's eyes twinkled with her amusement.

"I see. And your sisters' names?"

Holland matched the woman's grin. "Ireland, London, France—we call her Frankie—and Carolina."

"How unique. I like it," Violet stated with a nod. "Very creative."

The woman's teacup rattled a bit as she lifted it to her lips for a sip, and Holland set the cookie aside for the time being.

"Come with me."

Holland froze in the act of sweetening her tea, and when she saw Violet getting to her feet, she hurried to stand and move to the woman's side, gently grasping her arm to steady her.

"Thank you, dear."

Violet led the way into the stunning home, through the living area to a sitting room off of what Holland assumed was the master suite. "That's the desk?"

"Yes."

"It's breathtaking."

"Yes, I suppose it is. Do you feel it appropriate for the auction?"

"Oh, my goodness, yes. I think it will do very well. Thank you, Violet."

"It won't be missed," the woman stated with a firm shake of her head. "In fact," she said, turning to look at Holland, "I would like to hire your services like my friend Margaret did. When I emptied the desk, I stumbled across some… memories. They made me realize I have quite a few things that make me think of unpleasant times, and I no longer want them."

"I'm sure my company would send a repres—"

"No, dear. I will only do it if you handle the account. I'm comfortable with you."

Holland faltered. She had a full plate with more than a few side plates to juggle. Taking on Violet as a client meant tripling down and then some. "I'm… not sure of the time-frame you have in mind. I just returned from an extended work trip and planned to take some time off to deal with the auction and London's wedding preparations, as well as the baby shower planned for Ireland. Things are a bit chaotic for me at the moment."

"The auction is still a month away."

"Yes, but—"

"And the wedding is?"

"Uh, mid-April, right after the auction. The wedding is a week beyond that."

Violet smiled.

"That's plenty of time, my dear. Especially if you stay here. Wilmington traffic is such a bother these days."

"Mrs. Bane—"

"Violet, dear."

"Violet, I live in Carolina Cove. If I were to take the job, it's not that far to drive home. There's no reason for me to intrude."

"Bah. There's no intrusion. I'd welcome the company. It gets lonely in this big old house. My sons rarely visit, my grandchildren even less so now that they're grown with families of their own. You'd keep me company as we cycle through some unpleasant memories, and I'd be sure to let your company know how valuable you are to them."

Holland faltered yet again. Because of the mention of unpleasant memories. That piqued her interest in the extreme. But more than that… She'd worked with a lot of extremely wealthy people over the years, but getting that kind of boost from the Bane matriarch would go a long way in obtaining the best assignments in the future. And when percentages of listings were factored into her commission bonuses… "Of course. I'll let my company know. You'll need to sign a contract, and we can get started on Mon—"

"Tomorrow."

"Tomorrow?"

"I'm not getting any younger, dear."

Okay, then. So much for the weekend. "Tomorrow it is."

TWO HOURS after her meeting with Violet Bane, Holland entered her home in Carolina Cove and found Carolina standing in the kitchen, kissing her boyfriend, Silas. Her youngest sister pulled back and flashed Holland a smile but didn't loose her hold on Silas's broad shoulders.

"Guess what?" Carolina said.

"What?"

"We just got booked to house-sit for a last-minute getaway. We leave tomorrow for Aruba. Can you believe it? Aruba!"

"That's great," Holland said. "Are you taking Lucy?"

"Yeah, it's only a four-day assignment. To *Aruba!*"

Holland laughed at Carolina's excitement, more than a little pleased at her sister's luck. It had been hard for Carolina to take a step back and change her thinking regarding her desire to be a professional international house sitter once Silas and his daughter, Lucy, had entered her life. Her dreams had nearly ended their relationship, but Carolina had regrouped and countered the opportunity by getting Silas to agree to go with her on shorter assignments as his work schedule allowed. The compromise fed Carolina's dreams and desire for travel while allowing them to provide the stability Lucy needed and Silas's job demanded. "Little Lucy is getting a lot of great travel experience for that new passport of hers."

Lucy was a brainiac. A for-real child genius, and while taking her out of school might be problematic for some children, for Lucy it seemed to accelerate her desire to learn. The kid was probably tucked upstairs on Carolina's bed researching Aruba and all its marine life while waiting on dinner.

"I know, right? And I know I can definitely use some time on a sugar-sand beach. The owners want us to pet and plant sit and they have their own private beach access."

"I don't think I've seen you this excited," Silas said, dropping a kiss atop Carolina's head before releasing her to move toward the fridge.

"Aruba, ba-by!" Carolina said with a grin. "Where have you been, Holl?"

Holland dropped her bag on the couch and took off her heels, carrying them to the stairs so she wouldn't forget to take them up when she went to pack for her stay. "I had a charity donation meeting that turned into a client meeting. The woman insists I stay with her while I gather the information for the listings, but it's right on the IC, so it's not a hardship."

"Niiice. You gonna do it?"

"Well, I like eating and being employed, so, yeah. She's a young ninety-four and a little lonely, and it could mean a nice-sized bonus."

"I believe in you," Carolina said, grinning. "You've got this. What's the house like?"

"*Stunning*. Amazing views, amazing furnishings. It'll be fun to see what treasures she's ready to part with."

"What's her name?" Silas asked.

Carolina immediately shook her head. "She can tell you but then she'd have to kill you."

Holland laughed but shrugged. "Yeah, that pretty much sums it up. Privacy policy. Generals are okay but I can't give specifics."

"Gotcha," Silas said, lowering himself to the couch. "I didn't realize your job was a real thing until Carolina told me about it."

"It's never boring, that's for sure," Holland said. She liked her job. Loved the travel aspect and getting to play with, stay on, momentarily wear, fly in, drive, or otherwise research the usually insanely expensive items people no longer wanted. Over the years, she'd been able to satisfy her expensive tastes without spending a dime. "I'm going to go pack."

"Dinner's almost ready."

"Okay, but just a salad for me. I had some sort of cookie that was probably a billion calories but surprisingly filling."

"Fancy. Try to bring some of those home when you can," Carolina said, grinning. "What? I can't even have a cookie? Tough crowd."

Holland laughed as she climbed the stairs. "I'll see what I can do but no promises."

Minutes later she entered her bedroom and removed the suitcase she'd just placed in the closet two days ago when she'd returned from a job in Brazil. She hadn't planned on leaving again for a while, but staying at Violet's during the job wasn't out of the norm.

She went back to her closet and took a quick survey, deciding on multiple tops and slacks, a few nice dresses, one fancy dress just to prepare for any major surprise, and several sweaters and a jacket that could be worn inter-changeably. Holland dropped those onto the bed to roll later and moved to her armoire to get a bathing suit and cover-up. Homes with heated pools were definitely a favorite of hers and a treat she wouldn't pass up. She also added a packable but cold-weather coat for free time when she could sit under their gazebo at the end of the dock.

Needing only the last-minute essentials, she pulled her laptop from the bag she'd carried to Violet's and settled behind the desk. A search of Violet Bane's name left her scrolling through images of Violet as a younger woman. Charities and boards, fundraisers. Lots of volunteer work.

The beautiful wife of an influential man who had passed on six years ago.

Holland kept clicking and found pictures of Violet's two sons as well as a few grandchildren and great-grandchildren.

She hesitated, then used the mouse to slide over into the thousands of articles featuring the family's political, business, and personal dealings as well as a few scandals back in the day that would barely be a blip on the radar in today's world.

"Dinner's ready!"

Holland closed the laptop with a soft click. Violet's comment about the lack of family visits made Holland sad. Someone had once told her there was nothing more invisible than an old woman, and for the first time, it sank in that one day she could look around and find herself in Violet's shoes—if she was lucky enough to have a family at all.

Holland leaned back in the chair and rubbed her temple with her fingertips in a sad attempt to ease the tension. It wasn't unusual for a family member or assistant to contact her company about the prospect of listing items. But Violet had made the call herself and something nagged Holland enough to make her wonder… if Violet was intent on selling her things, why was she doing it all alone?

Chapter 2

The following evening, Maximilian Bane squeezed through the elevator doors of his grandmother's home before the doors completely opened and stalked into the room. "Nan? Sally?"

Silence. The older maid was usually near his grandmother, so Max set off to find the women somewhere in the six-thousand-square-foot home. A search of the second floor produced no one, and since the third-floor rooms were now guest rooms, he took the stairs to the lower level, thinking maybe they hadn't heard him let himself inside.

He moved through the house with purposeful strides, trying hard to distance himself from the anger and tension riding him. When he'd called to check on his grandmother, she'd mentioned her decision to sell items given to her by his grandfather over the years. The news had been such a shock that he'd changed the location of a business deal in the works to Wilmington and hopped a plane from New York. The move had angered his potential buyer because of the last-minute change in plans, but it couldn't be helped.

Someone had to check on his grandmother, and that someone was him unless he wanted to alert his family and potentially have his greedy relatives descending on her. He wanted to check things out first. See what had caused the sudden decision and if there was something he could do to help.

Max stalked to the back of the house. A sharp gasp drew his attention to a blond woman on the other side of the room… taking photos? "Who are you? What are you doing?"

She blinked at him, the hand that had flown to her chest in her fright from his arrival drawing his attention as he noted the lack of ring. He moved toward her, taking in a beautiful face and figure. "Give me that."

"What? No."

"Hand it over. Now."

"Will you just— Hey, hands off! Who are *you*?"

Max stopped and stared down into the woman's brown eyes, noting the flecks of gold and dark green in the unusual sienna-colored depths. He deftly plucked the phone from her hand and turned the screen to see it.

"That's mine!"

The last photo was a smudged image of her hand probably taken when he'd caught her snooping and startled her, but the ones before that were of his grandmother's things. So she was the one behind this mess? "What do you hope to gain from this?"

The woman crossed her arms over her ample front and tilted her head to one side. "Well, I suppose the goal is doing my job," she said, her tone laden with barely veiled sarcasm. "My name is Holland Cohen. Who are *you* and why—"

She attempted to snatch the phone from his hand but he held it out of her reach.

"—are you stealing my phone?"

"What job?"

"How about you answer my questions first? I told you my name. Do you have one?"

He narrowed his gaze on her even more. Did she really not recognize him? It wasn't a matter of vanity or ego, but there were few people who didn't these days. "Maximilian Bane. Violet is my grandmother."

"Oh."

She blinked but other than that she didn't show any signs of recognizing him as anything except a relative.

"Well, nice to meet you, I suppose. Now will you please give me my phone before you crush it?"

Her added *I suppose* drew a huff of laughter from him. For the first time, he realized he gripped her phone to the point of pain, the edges of the protective case digging into his fingers and hand like a knife. He relaxed his grip but didn't hand it over to her just yet. "You work for my grandmother?"

He knew what Nan had told him over the phone, but he wanted to get Holland Cohen's take on things since it was obvious his grandmother hadn't warned her of his potential arrival.

"Yes. I mean, no, but yes."

When he waited for her to continue, she inhaled as though drawing on some secret source of patience.

"I work for a company Mrs. Bane hired. Due to our confidentiality terms, if you want more information than that, you'll have to ask her yourself. My phone. Please." She held out her palm and waited.

"What's the name of the company?"

She gave him the name and he tucked the information back for later. He would investigate both Holland Cohen and her company before the evening was over. Until then… "Where is my grandmother?"

"Someone called to inform her of a medical emergency involving a friend. Sally accompanied Violet to the hospital."

"And she just left you here?"

The woman straightened to her full height, which still left her about six inches short of his six feet two. Her squared shoulders and lifted chin told him he'd struck a nerve.

"My credentials are exemplary, I can assure you. And they include a thorough background check. You can inquire about them with my boss if you like."

Her eyes glittered with her upset that he would question her morals, and he found himself drawn to the way the golden flecks in her brown eyes darkened to molten glass. "I mean no offense. I simply don't want someone taking advantage of my grandmother."

"Well, on that, we can agree."

Max held her gaze a long moment before he forced himself to break eye contact to look around the room. Why sell anything? The room, the house, was fine. Were all women so materialistic that they had to change decor every year? His mother, his ex-girlfriend… They both demanded the latest fashions and furnishings, no matter the cost or the waste.

Max turned on his heel and headed across the room to the lower-level kitchen. "I'm hungry. Have you eaten?"

"Really?"

He glared at her from across the room, wishing he could shake off the bad mood he was in. "Look, Ms. Cohen, I'm sorry for yelling at you. My grandmother mentioned her plans last night when I called and it created a great deal of concern."

"Apology accepted," she said simply, warily.

"So why is my grandmother wanting to sell her things? Time to redecorate?"

Holland joined him in the kitchen area but kept the island bar between her and his bad mood.

"Like I said, you'll have to ask her for more information. I only told you what I did so you wouldn't call the police and have me arrested for trespassing. I'm sure your grandmother will explain things when she returns."

Not the answer he wanted considering it meant babysitting his grandmother's guest. "I see. Well, then until then, it's just you and me, Ms. Cohen."

VIOLET'S GRANDSON belonged on a magazine cover. Tall, dark, and handsome, Maximilian Bane wore faded jeans and a black pullover that emphasized his black hair and the slightest bit of silver sparkling in the depths.

He'd startled her earlier, appearing out of nowhere in soft, silent boots that probably cost the earth but appeared to be favorites given their worn state. A sexy bit of scruff lined his chin and jawline, and she wondered if he always wore a beard or if it was due to whatever stress had put the shadows under his forest-green eyes.

While he searched the fridge to ward off his hunger, she continued her perusal and tried to slow her racing heart. The man had long, lean fingers, clean nails, but as she watched him brace his weight against the marble countertop and lean low to peer into the cabinets to continue his search, she noted his hands looked to be those of a man used to manual labor, a definite surprise considering his last name. Based on the photos of the family she'd seen online last night, she wouldn't have guessed the Bane men to be the hands-on type. "The fridge upstairs is better stocked, I believe," she said when he frowned.

"So I've gathered."

His green-eyed gaze locked on hers and a tingle shot through her. Holland frowned and shifted her weight. Surely she'd imagined that, right?

Because as far as she knew, that only happened in romance novels—or to her sisters. Carolina had told her, when Silas first kissed her, he'd curled her toes. Were curling toes and tingles anywhere close to the same thing?

You're obviously overworked if you think a man barking at you is sexy in any way.

"Care to join me?"

She blinked to awareness and found he'd noticed her watching him. To avoid his gaze, she glanced at her watch and noted the time. "I hope everything is okay with Violet's friend. I got the impression it was quite serious."

"How long have they been gone?"

"They left around two." Not long after she had arrived.

"I'll call Sally and check on things if they haven't returned in another hour or so."

He cared for her. That much was apparent in his tone and the frustrated way he stated the fact. "She seems pretty spry. And her mental state is something everyone hopes to have at her age."

He lifted his hands and ran them over his head as though to relieve tension.

"The family has been trying to get her to move back to Virginia for years but she won't hear of it."

Holland turned toward the windows and the view of the IC and the Atlantic beyond. "Can you blame her? Getting older is hard enough, but for someone as sharp as your grandmother appears, I don't imagine she likes having people ordering her around like a child."

His gaze sharpened on her once again and Holland bit her lower lip. *Keep the comments to yourself, Holl. Do your job, go home. The hired help doesn't have an opinion, remember?*

But would she have a job after Max talked to his grandmother? Or would he change her mind and insist on breaking the contract? She might not have wanted the job in the beginning, but Violet was such a sweet woman that Holland wanted to do what she could to help.

She inhaled and sighed. Until Violet tempered her grandson's questions, Holland had a feeling her work was done for the day. No use moving ahead if the job ended as quickly as it had fallen into her lap.

The pool beckoned, but would she be able to enjoy it while Maximilian Bane was in the house? "While you find your dinner, I'll run upstairs and get one of my cards. Maybe then you'll see that I'm legit."

"You're staying here?"

"Your grandmother insisted on it. But it isn't an unusual request," she hastened to add.

His dark eyebrows pulled into a low frown.

"The card can wait. How about we both go find some dinner? I'm sure Sally has something prepared upstairs. She always does."

Maximilian moved around the island separating them and held out his hand to indicate she should go before him. Holland figured it was his way of keeping an eye on her, making sure she didn't disappear with one of the family heirlooms he was apparently so worried about.

She felt awkward walking upstairs beside Violet's grandson, but once at the top, she stepped away and let him take the lead as they headed toward the kitchen.

"I dropped my bag in the blue room when I looked for Nan and Sally, but I didn't realize you were staying here. I can move it if that's the room you're in."

"Um. It is, actually. Violet said it has the best views of the sunrise. I can pack up and—"

"No. Anything better than a dirt floor is fine."

She laughed but the sound emerged sounding awkward and tense. Like he'd ever slept on a dirt floor.

Or… had he? There was something in his expression. Maybe he wasn't the rich pretty boy she'd first thought based on his name?

Holland worried her lower lip between her teeth, unsure of what she should do given the turn of events. Violet would no doubt rather spend time with her grandson, not have a stranger in her home. Should she leave? "She, um, didn't mention you were visiting when she asked me to stay."

"I hadn't planned on it. I called her last night because I was in New York on business, but when she mentioned selling the family silver, I thought it best to come check on things."

"Well, I'm sure she won't mind a visit, regardless of the reason. She's mentioned her family a lot. She misses them… you." *Yeah, remember that part about keeping your thoughts and Violet's reasons to yourself?*

Max—could she call him that?—turned toward the fridge once they reached the kitchen and opened the door.

"Success. Sally must have been working on it when they got the call. Looks like baked Parmesan chicken, salad, and some kind of veggies. A feast."

The sound of the elevator doors opening filled the area, and Violet and Sally soon appeared. Both women looked exhausted, but Violet especially so.

"Max! Oh, what a wonderful surprise. It's so good to see you."

Max moved toward his grandmother, towering over her when he gently grasped her hands in his.

"It's good to see you, too, Nan." He kissed Violet's cheek. "How are you?"

Violet's hand trembled as she patted her grandson's cheek. "Not a good day to ask, my love. Margaret didn't make it. She passed a little while ago after a stroke this morning."

Margaret? The woman Holland had listed and sold jewelry for. Margaret had attended the ladies' luncheon as well. "I'm so sorry, Mrs. Bane." Loss was hard, but harder still when the person was there, smiling and happy, days earlier.

"Violet, my dear. I told you, I don't stand on formality."

Max slid his arm around Violet's shoulders and clasped her to his side as though lending her strength.

"I'm sorry for your loss, Nan."

The woman's eyes filled with tears that quickly trickled down her cheeks before she lifted a wadded and already damp tissue to dab them away.

"It's something we must all prepare for one day," Violet said. "Sally's going to help me to my room. I'm sorry, children, but I want to lie down. Please eat and visit and enjoy yourselves. Holland, we will begin tomorrow."

"Whatever you like," Holland said quickly.

"I'll be back shortly to get dinner ready," Sally told them.

"No rush," Max said to the woman while lowering his head to kiss the top of his grandmother's head.

Holland watched, heart breaking, as the housekeeper walked slowly at Violet's side toward the hall that led toward the master suite. The difference between Violet yesterday and now was agonizing. Gone was the vibrant, determined woman full of grit and sass, and in her place was someone very aware of every moment and struggling with the depths of loss.

"Margaret and Nan have been friends a long time. Her first friend when my grandparents moved here."

Holland struggled to speak over the lump in her throat. "I think I should go home. Come back tomorrow."

"No. She would be upset if you left and blame me. Let her rest. When she wakes up, she'll need the distraction of you in the house. I'll give her some time before I bring up her decision to consign the items."

Max met her gaze and gave her a grim smile that didn't reach his eyes.

"Holland, I'll be in and out working on the business deal that brought me to the States, and I'm sure she would enjoy your company. It's the weekend. Don't change your plans just yet. Please."

Maybe if he hadn't said please. But he did say it and, with him staring at her the way that he did, the request left her nodding. "Okay. I'll stay the weekend."

She just wasn't sure if she had agreed because of the job she might no longer have, Violet's need for companionship, or her curiosity about Maximilian Bane but… she was staying.

Chapter 3

"Five daughters on a military base surrounded by soldiers. It's a wonder your father is sane," Max said, staring across the dinner table into Holland's beautiful brown eyes.

Sally had returned from getting his grandmother settled and delivered dinner shortly thereafter. And even though he'd only just met Holland Cohen, she'd quickly proven herself to be a woman worth a second look. Behind the blond hair and sienna-colored eyes was a sharp mind and confidence born of someone well educated and traveled.

"It wasn't a problem until Ireland and I discovered boys with accents," Holland said, smiling as she lifted her glass to her lips. "Then we had an entire base of big brothers who knew the colonel would have their hides if they saw us out and about where we weren't supposed to be."

He settled himself deeper into the dining chair and laced his fingers over his full stomach as he chuckled. "Your childhood sounds fun."

"It was. So many kids hated being a military brat but

we always had each other. Moving was just another adventure and new place to explore."

"How many countries?"

"How many have I been to? I've never sat down and counted. That's more Carolina's thing."

"The house sitter?"

Holland nodded. "You've got a good memory. Yes, the house sitter. She's the youngest and our parents settled in Carolina Cove around the time she was old enough to do all the stuff we older girls did. She feels like she's missed out on that and is determined to make up for it, so she has a map on her wall of places she wants to go."

"And what about you? Where would you like to go that you haven't traveled?"

"Oh, tough question."

He liked the way her lips curled at the corners. How her eyes sparkled with intent as she pondered her response.

"Well, there are places I'd like to go back to because they were so beautiful. Switzerland, for one. Austria. Pretty much any beach along the equator because of that sugar-white sand. And I've never been to Iceland but I'm told it's beautiful. What about you? Where would you love to go?"

"It's been a while since I've taken a vacation. I'm not sure."

"But you travel a lot?"

"I've done more than my share."

"You know, you've mentioned business a few times but I don't actually know what you do."

He liked that she didn't know. "I create start-ups, mostly." He was deliberately vague, but in a world where an internet search would provide more than she'd ever want to know about him, he didn't feel the need to tout his successes.

"What else?"

"What do you mean?"

"You don't get those hands from sitting behind a computer screen," she said, her head tilted to one side. "You do some pretty intense physical labor, and I'm guessing whatever it is, it's a labor of love."

Shock rolled through him at the astuteness of her observation and he stilled.

"My grandfather calls them workingman's hands. He always said they were a badge of honor."

Honor. Labor of love. At the start, the work had been a punishment given to him by his father when his privileged life had started to spiral out of control, but over time, things had changed. And so had he. "I'm not always locked away in a boardroom or behind a computer screen."

She had more questions. He could see it in her eyes. But she seemed content for the moment.

"Are you finished, Ms. Cohen?"

Sally's question drew Holland's attention away from him and Max released a breath he hadn't realized he held.

"Yes. Thank you, Sally. May I help you clear the dishes?"

"No, Ms. Cohen. You enjoy your evening."

His phone chimed and he flipped it over to check the screen. "Pardon me. I have to take this."

"Of course."

Max excused himself from the table and answered the call on his way to the door but not before taking a last look at Holland, her blond hair gleaming beneath the light. She smiled at Sally and asked about her day, and the softly spoken query visibly touched his grandmother's longtime employee and left him wondering if there wasn't more to Holland Cohen than just a pretty face. "Bane."

. . .

WITH SALLY BUSY CLEANING UP, Violet tucked away in bed for the night, and Max handling the business call, Holland felt at loose ends. Normally when staying at a residence, she was either working or out exploring in her downtime. But as she paced across her bedroom to the window and saw the sparkling blue water of the pool below, she decided to take advantage of the opportunity while she could. She needed a good workout and a swim would be perfect.

She moved to the dresser where she'd unpacked her swimsuits and settled on a simple black one-piece that held in her curves while giving her security to push herself in the water.

Suit on, hair braided, and coverup in place, she grabbed a towel from the stack Sally had given her earlier and opened the door to take a quick peek outside. No way did she want to risk running into Violet's handsome grandson. Bathing suit visuals weren't businesslike, after all.

Holland moved through the two-thousand-square-foot third floor of the house to the elevator, determined that once she got her workout in she'd do a lot more research on the Banes. One in particular.

The elevator doors opened with a whisper of sound, and once again she crossed the lower-level expanse to enter the living area, moving on through the screened-in patio, and outside. The temperature had dropped considerably and she hurried to strip off the cover-up.

Steam rose from the water's surface and she dove in with barely a splash. A shiver raced through her as she was swallowed up by the warmth. She broke the surface with a gasp and flipped onto her back to stare up at the sky, performing a lazy backstroke until she reached the edge. From there she flipped and pushed off, maintaining a fairly doable speed for several laps until she kicked it up another notch. By the time she finished, she was completely out of breath and hugging the edge of the pool while she regained her equilibrium enough to get out.

The heat of the pool did much to combat the cold breeze, but she dried off as quickly as possible and donned her cover-up. The hot tub beckoned, but after the swim, she was ready for a shower and bed.

She let herself back into the house as quietly as possible, double-checking that she properly locked the door behind her.

"That was impressive."

Holland lifted her head and turned to find Max regarding her from the doorway of the billiard room. He held a pool cue in his hands, his gaze direct as it swept over her from the top of her wet head to her bare feet. "Um. Hi. Violet said I earlier that I was welcome to use the pool."

"I heard. Do you swim a lot? That was some impressive speed."

He'd watched her? She felt her skin begin to flush. "Oh, thanks. I used to. High school and college teams. I usually finished last but it was fun."

Max smiled and she realized she liked seeing him smile. It made him more handsome, less like a man troubled by the world and her presence in his grandmother's home, and more like the thirtysomething he was. "Do you swim?"

"Not anymore."

Something about the way he said it caught her attention, but given the weight of the words and the tone, she knew better than to press for more information.

"It's early yet. Would you be interested in a game?" he asked with a tilt of his head toward the table.

She stared up at him. Interested? Yeah. She was. But games weren't her thing and she knew from experience wealthy men tended to view her as "game" material. A nice dinner date, perhaps arm candy for lack of a better descriptive… but she didn't have the background and upbringing for men with names like Bane.

The fact she was drawn to Maximilian Bane surprised her more than anything. It had been quite some time since she'd met a man who remotely intrigued her enough to consider practicing her flirting skills, much less wonder what it would be like if he'd step closer, lower his head, and—

"I suppose not. You're shivering."

She clutched the damp towel a little higher and nodded. "I-I… should change first, but, yeah. Sure. That is, if you don't mind waiting a bit." So much for going to bed early. But even she knew she'd probably just stare at the computer doing research on the man in front of her, and if that was the case, why not ask the source?

"I don't mind."

She managed a smile and unglued her feet from the tile floor. "Okay, then. I'll be back."

Her heart pounded in her chest the entire walk to the elevator and the ride to the third floor. Which was crazy because she wasn't a young girl getting asked to sit at the lunch table with her first crush. At thirty-three, dating wasn't new. But this wasn't a date and she still felt this way, and that, well, that was the issue. She'd turned down the last couple of invitations she'd received due to sheer lack of interest. So why accept this one?

Because you don't want him standing between you and your bonus?

No. That wasn't true. If Violet decided to change her mind, so be it.

Holland rushed into her room and stripped down.

Max was bored, passing the time in a houseful of

women, and she was the only one relatively close to him in age. It wasn't interest that had drawn the invitation but necessity unless he planned to spend the remainder of the evening alone or go out for some fun in an area not yet awake for the summer tourist season.

She rummaged through the drawers holding the clothes she'd brought with her and found a pair of leggings. Thankfully she'd brought a super-soft turquoise top she loved. Was she trying too hard not to impress? Tough call. But she didn't want to look frumpy, either.

"Ugh, why is this so difficult?" she muttered, yanking on the leggings and donning the shirt because, in all of her debating, she wasted precious time. Dressed, she went to the bathroom. Her hair was best left braided until she could wash out the salt, but she did a light touch-up on her mascara and lip gloss and deemed herself as passable.

Her phone chimed and she glanced at the screen. Ireland.

Heard you scored a local assignment. Doing okay?

Yes. Fine. Heading downstairs to schmooze a bit.

After all, Ireland didn't need to know specifics. Or that Max had nothing to do with the job itself.

Fun! Any single, good-looking men involved?

Her sister would have to ask that question, wouldn't she? Ever since Ireland had fallen in love again, she'd been on a mission to set Holland up with one of her husband's friends, but thankfully the timing had never worked out.

Client is 92. Enough said, she texted back. Because if she opened the door by mentioning a super-sexy, presumably single Max, Holland knew she'd probably have to answer a bevy of texts from all of her sisters instead of heading downstairs to get to know the man in question.

She left her phone behind in her room and made her

way to the elevator, all too aware of that pulse-racing thing repeating itself. She heard the billiard balls clanking together as she approached the room, and when she walked inside, Max racked them.

"Heard the elevator," he said simply.

"So I see."

"You any good?"

"We'll have to find out." It had been weeks since she'd played, but she and all of her sisters were good at the game thanks to way too many hours on bases with little to do and a father determined his girls would be able to hold their own in a male-driven world.

"You break."

Mmm. He was playing the gentleman, giving her the advantage. It could help. Because while she wasn't a man-trashing feminist, she refused to deliberately lose just because it might bruise his ego. She also had a feeling Max was the type of man who'd be able to tell if she threw the game, which meant a fifty-fifty chance of him losing respect for her for doing so.

She chose a cue and chalked up, forcing herself to take a breath and slow her heart rate. Steady hands were needed.

Holland did a few practice slides of the cue and exhaled slowly once more before letting the cue strike. The crack of sound seemed deafening and she worried that she might have disturbed Violet upstairs, but given the size of the house, it undoubtedly wasn't an issue.

Several balls hit the pockets and she had a choice. "Solids." She'd always looked better in solids than stripes.

As she moved around the table and chose her next target, she felt Max's eyes on her.

"I get the feeling you're better at this than you let on."

His words brought a curl to her lips and she lined up her shot. And got it.

Max chuckled, the sound wry.

"Glad I didn't make a bet with you on this."

Mmm. That could be interesting. "It's not too late."

His gaze narrowed on her.

"That sounds like a challenge. What do you have in mind?"

Chapter 4

She rounded the table with a thoughtful perusal of her options, not only of the next shot but of a worthy bet that wouldn't seem too over-the-top. "Let's see. Ah. Got it," she said, smiling at him. "If I win, you tell me why you don't swim anymore. And if you win… I don't know, I'll give you five bucks."

"Five bucks? No."

"Ten?"

"The answer is worth way more."

She smiled at his words, aimed, and took her shot. Nailed it with a satisfactory slam in the pocket. "So what's it worth?"

"Dinner. Your favorite place."

Dang. Here she'd thought she wouldn't be throwing a game. "That seems a little one-sided."

"I guess that depends on who wins."

"Okay, then. Deal." And because she couldn't make it totally obvious that she wanted him to win, she lined up the next shot and nailed it but then scratched because she deliberately didn't put a spin on it.

Max lifted his thick eyebrows high but didn't comment as he fished the white ball from the pocket and moved around the table.

"Excuse me," he said, squeezing by her on the side closest to the wall.

She got a whiff of his cologne and liked the scent. Not too strong and not put on with a heavy hand. Double win, in her humble opinion. So many men were just as bad as women when it came to the proper use of scent, leaving a lung-clogging cloud behind them in their wake.

Holland turned to watch him take his spot at the end of the table, once again wondering what kind of work Max did that created the rough look of his hands. He took his shot and made it and she studied his technique. Her father had told her once that she could learn a lot about a man by the way he played pool or cards. A simple study would prove if he was reckless or impatient or deliberate, thoughtful, and took his time.

Max was the latter. Every shot came after quiet contemplation and probably more than a few physics calculations in his head as he overtook her score and gained the lead with some difficult shots she wasn't sure she could've made. Maybe she wouldn't have to throw the game to score dinner with a handsome man after all.

A quietness settled over the table as the game contin-ued. Max finally missed and gave her another chance, but she missed by a hair and gave him the advantage yet again. Back and forth they played until Max lined up his final shot. "Did you hear that?" she asked, tilting her head as though hearing some faraway noise. "I think someone just called for us. We should go check it out."

"Nope," Max said with a gorgeous grin. "Didn't hear a thing."

He took the shot. Made it with all of the quiet deliberation and intent he'd played with throughout the game and slowly straightened. "Hmm. Looks like you owe me dinner."

She stared at the table as though pondering the meaning of life. "Double or nothing?"

His low chuckle brought a smile to her lips and a shiver raced through her. It was all too easy to imagine that low, sexy chuckle sounding in her ear as he pulled her close and…

Daydreaming much there, Holl?

"Dinner. Maybe some dancing."

Dancing? She did so like a man who would at least sway back and forth to the music and not sit there like a log. "Swimming is like dancing, you know."

He moved close to her and took the pool cue from her hand.

"Debatable."

"What? No. It totally is. There's movement and speed, timing. It all factors in."

She watched as he carefully laid the cues atop the table.

"I suppose one could see it that way."

She'd come downstairs barefoot in her rush because, at the time, she'd been so worried about what to wear that she hadn't actually thought about shoes. With Max standing so close, she had to tilt her head back even more due to her lack of height.

Had she always had a thing for tall men? Because right now she totally did. Max's height made her feel small and feminine and…

Slow it down, girlie.

"It's late and that swim wiped me out. I should go," she said, taking a small step back. "It's been a long week and I'm still a little jet-lagged."

"I should turn in as well. Same reason."

Max hit the elevator button and waited for her to precede him once the doors opened.

"You played a good game."

"Thanks. So did you."

"I had good incentive. It isn't every day I get to go out with a beautiful pool shark."

"Yes, well, you may not think so when I take you to my favorite place for dinner."

"Another challenge?"

"No. Just not everyone's cup of tea."

"I look forward to it."

They exchanged a glance that sucked the air from her lungs and made Holland question why she played with fire. The doors opened, and for the first time, Holland realized she and Max apparently shared the third floor, because he wasn't just walking her to her room. "Good night."

If her sisters were there, they'd have some comment about cutting the tension with a knife or the air sizzling. Carolina would be starry-eyed, for sure. Truth be told, Holland wasn't much better at the moment. The tension was there, the chemistry so elusive to her until now blazing out of control. But insta-love was insta-lust more often than not, and she didn't go for such things. She held herself to a higher standard. Intimacy—sex— for her it was all about connection, and until she had one, the handsome Max would remain at arm's length. No exceptions.

"Good night, Holland. Sweet dreams."

She bit her lower lip and walked to her room on trembling legs, leaning hard against the door once she was inside.

Dannng.

She'd told Carolina that she'd never had a man make her toes curl from a kiss. And she still hadn't. But just then? Max had made her toes curl just from the searing look he'd given her before walking away. He could've pressed her for more. Could've tried to kiss her. Could've done any number of things most men at his age and in his position of power and wealth would've done—had done—to attempt to gain access to her bed.

But he hadn't. And her interest in him ratcheted up several more notches because of it.

Dinner with Max was going to be interesting.

HOLLAND SPENT the next morning and part of the afternoon following Violet through the three-story home, making notes on the items Violet wanted to sell, even though Holland wondered if Violet's decision to list the many pieces would be undone once Max sat down with his grandmother to talk about her reasons why.

Included in the growing list of items was a silver centerpiece Holland guessed worth fifty thousand or so, as well as a silver tea set that should bring a minimum of thirty. There was also a silver vase circa 1882 worth another twenty thousand. No doubt these were the silver heirlooms Max had referred to, and only three of the many pieces Violet had Sally retrieve from storage and display on the dining room table for Holland to look over while the elderly woman retreated to her private rooms once more to rest.

Holland wandered through the house a second time, wondering if she could list the items in good conscience after having witnessed the depths of Violet's grief. Perhaps she could claim a family emergency and reschedule her stay?

Holland found herself in the sitting area on the second floor near the desk Violet had donated to the charity auction. She paused to take a more in-depth look at the desk, only then noticing the maker's mark underneath the right front side. She made a notation about the find and took a photograph for the auction booklet, knowing it would increase the value.

Holland's mental battle of whether or not to decline Violet as a client continued as she photographed the desk. She opened drawers to show the inside, then pulled it away from the wall to get the sides and back. A small noise sounded when she removed her fingers from the back and she gasped.

Did I break it?

She moved to the side of the desk and saw a section of wood sticking out beyond the rest. She gently pressed it and it went back into place. A secret panel?

Holland moved the desk farther into the room and pressed the section again, only this time when it extended, she gently pulled the piece to find a hidden compartment with papers tucked inside. "What on earth?"

She quickly looked the desk over, pressing and gently pulling anything that might remotely be a second hiding place, but didn't find anything. Still, the one in the back waited for exploration, and she rushed around the desk yet again to remove the papers, taking her time so they wouldn't rip.

They were quite old. The paper thin. Letters. With no return addresses. All were addressed to "My flower," Holland whispered.

Violet?

Knowing she shouldn't intrude, yet unable to stem the curiosity inside of her, Holland carefully untied the aged purple ribbon holding the letters bound and quickly counted them. Twenty-two.

Holland sank to the floor where she knelt and carefully opened the one on top.

My flower, how I miss you. I wait impatiently for the moments I can see you. For the long day to end so you return from school and I can catch just a glimpse of your beauty. To see my heart walking toward me for precious seconds. Even though we dare not speak aloud in public, I see the love in your eyes and I am humbled.

The letter was signed *Your prince.*

Holland exhaled slowly and battled the lure, knowing she shouldn't continue reading something so private but unable to stop herself. She carefully returned the letter to the tiny paper envelope and retrieved another one, praying for forgiveness.

My flower, you looked so beautiful today. You wore yellow and stood in the sunlight of your mother's window and I watched from outside, barely able to draw breath. You were light and beauty in a dark world. I miss you. I pray for the moments we spend together when we hide away from prying eyes. I pray for the day we can be together.

One after another, Holland read the pages. The first eighteen of them were from a man very much in love, but the last four…

Holland lifted her hand to her mouth when she unfolded the next letter and scanned the delicate feminine writing.

My prince, it has been less than a day since they came and took you away from me. I am heartbroken, sickened by this cruel world. I have not eaten or slept. I cry constantly. The pain is unbearable. I can't imagine what you're going through. What they will do to you. Return to me as soon as you can, my love. I will wait for you always. Your flower

What? Where did he go? Who took him?

Holland flipped the envelope over but there was nothing to tell her what she wanted to know. She kept reading but it was much of the same. The letters written but never sent. Full of fear, worry, anguish.

Why won't you write to me?

Are you alive?

I dream of you and pray you are safe.

Oh, the news! The news is so terrible. I do not believe they are treating you well, otherwise you would be able to contact me. My heart, where are you? Please, hear me calling you.

Holland hesitated before lifting the last letter. Uncertain she wanted to know what it said because there were no more to follow. Her hands trembled, her muscles tense from the emotionally charged statements.

My prince, it has been a year since I've seen or heard from you. My broken heart has not yet healed but my father insists I marry because I have turned eighteen. You were my first love, my only love. Mine will be a marriage of convenience, a business transaction born of old men in suits craving power and connection. Bane, Bane! I hate the name Bane! They know nothing of love. My father does not understand my sacred vows to you whispered in the light of the moon, but I know wherever you are, you feel my anguish. You feel my love. I remember your kisses. How you made me ache with longing for you. Where are you, my prince? My beautiful prince.

If you can come for me before May third, please, my love, do. We will run away together and keep going until we find a place that will accept us. My love, my love, where are you? My heart is forever yours. I do not wish this marriage. I do not want it. I am tempted to run away but where would I go? Still, I do not want to be tied to a man I do not love. My prince, please come for me. Please, save me.

"Holland?"

Max's heavy footfalls thudded across the floor as he rushed toward her.

"What's wrong? Why are you shaking?"

She sniffled and lowered the hand held to her mouth out of her shock. She blinked and forced a smile, feeling silly and yet completely wrecked. "I shouldn't have read them. I'm sorry."

"Read what? Where did you get that?"

She shook her head and sniffled again, lifting and waving the letter she held. "From a hidden drawer in the back of the desk. They're *heartbreaking*."

Max knelt on the floor beside her, reaching for the letter she held.

"My prince?"

"They're mostly from him. But the last few are from her because he was taken somewhere by force and she writes to him in her grief. Do you know anything about these? Who wrote them? Read them in order," she said, quickly flipping the stack to hand to him one by one.

Max quickly read through the letters, the silence between them growing. "Max?" she asked once he'd finished.

"My grandmother," he said, his voice low as he waved the last letter in the air. "That's Nan's handwriting."

"Oh." The air left Holland's lungs in a rush. It hurt to think of the woman writing such passionate and loving letters to someone only to have lost him. "Who was her prince?"

"I don't know."

Holland gathered up the letters and the ribbon tying them. "Max… I'm sorry. I shouldn't have read them but when I found them… I'm sure it's disconcerting. Especially the part about your grandparents' marriage."

"Yeah."

"I'm sure she grew to love your grandfather with time."

"Yeah. I mean, I hope so. But reading these makes me want to know more about how things came about between her and my grandfather. Where and when those took place."

She leaned against the wall behind her. "I'm sure. I want to know more about the boy. Who was he? Where did they take him and why? What happened to him? I have so many questions."

"Me, too." Max stood and held out his hand to help her up. "I say we go find out."

Chapter 5

Max wasn't sure what to think as he and Holland walked through the house. His mind ran the gamut from wondering if his grandmother had taken part in an illicit affair to thinking maybe he was wrong and the handwriting wasn't hers.

They found his grandmother in the living room, a thick book open on her lap. "Nan?"

She pressed a finger to the page as though to hold her place and looked up at them with a smile. "Hello, dear. I didn't hear you come home. Holland, Sally said you were taking photos of the desk. Did you get what you needed for the auction?"

"Uh, yes. I did."

"Nan." Max lifted the letters he'd taken from Holland to carry and watched as his grandmother's gaze lowered. She looked confused for a moment before the color left her face.

"Violet? Are you all right?"

Holland rushed to his grandmother's side and lowered herself to the edge of the couch beside her.

"I'm fine, dear. I just wasn't expecting… Where did those… The desk? *That's* where I put them. I hid them so long ago I couldn't remember where I'd put them. I searched and searched. I thought Leland had found them, destroyed them."

Max moved closer to them, handing the letters over to his grandmother's outstretched hands. "Nan, we have questions."

"You read them?"

"I'm sorry," Holland said. "It's my fault. I found them and I was so curious that I read the first one and then… I sincerely apologize, Violet, but I couldn't stop. They were so beautiful. So full of love."

Max hefted a club chair up and moved it closer to the couch, settling across from his grandmother. "Nan, who was he? When was this?"

His grandmother stared down at the letters, her hands shaking as she smoothed her fingertips across the surface of the one on top.

"Many, many years ago."

"Nan, come on. We're adults here. Granddad is gone. What's the story behind those?"

"I've brought your tea," Sally said. "I'll leave this and get more cups."

The woman left the tray on the coffee table and returned to the kitchen. Moments later she was back again, her gaze curious as she spotted the letters. "Mrs. Bane, are those…?"

"Yes. Oh, Sally, Holland found them."

"We've looked for those for the last three years. She'd given up hope," Sally said, alerting Max to the fact that Sally had kept silent about yet another family secret.

"Who are they from, Nan?"

"Aki. His name was Akihiro Tadashi. He and his father

were our gardeners. We met in 1941, when Aki was seventeen. Oh, what a wonderful year we had together. We would sneak away and picnic by the lake. Read poetry and talk for hours, dreaming…"

Nan's expression shifted, changed to a faraway look and place where she was no longer in the room with them but… him.

Max stared at his grandmother, waiting for her to continue. "Nan?"

"It was such a wonderful year," Violet whispered again, her eyes filling with tears.

Sally poured three cups of tea and lifted one for Violet but his grandmother shook her head. "No, thank you, dear."

"May I stay?" Sally asked. "Hear the story again?"

"Of course. We've been together a long time," Violet said to him. "And Sally has been by my side through so much."

"I wouldn't want to be anywhere else," the woman stated softly, moving to the second club chair closest to Holland.

"Nan? What happened?"

"Aki wanted to study medicine. He was so bright, and he knew so much about herbs and plants because of his father. I loved him the moment I saw him. He said he fell in love with me just as quickly. I'm not sure that's true.

"My parents didn't fare well during the Depression but continued to live the lifestyle they were accustomed to in the years following. It wasn't long before they faced complete ruin, and by then my heart was taken. These," she said, her wrinkled hands smoothing over the letters on her lap, "were from him. Are what's left of the many, many letters he sent to me. One a day, for the year we were together. Aki made me laugh, brought me flowers. Made me perfume from the petals. We knew my family wouldn't approve of me marrying the gardener's son, so we planned to run away together."

Holland stretched out a hand and covered his grandmother's.

"He sounds like a very special young man."

"He was. He was my prince."

A smile lightened the severity of his grandmother's features, softening the lines and wrinkles.

"That's what his name meant. Shining prince. But while we made plans and dreamed of the future, the Japanese bombed Pearl Harbor. The war changed everything."

Holland sucked in a breath, her eyes filling with tears. Max watched her, charmed by her response as much as he was by the sight of her sitting on the floor sniffling after she'd read the letters. Holland had a huge heart, one she should probably protect more, but at the moment, he was glad that she didn't, because it distracted him from yet another family scandal hidden by the years that had passed since.

"The Japanese population was concentrated mostly out west. But everyone knew about Aki and his father working for us, and the officials came and took them away. The camps in the Midwest weren't ready yet, so they sent them all the way from Virginia to California. That morning Aki was there with me, and the next moment, he was gone. I didn't get a letter from him that day. I never heard from him again."

Max heard Sally sniffle and glanced at her to see her wiping away tears. Holland's eyes glittered but she didn't let them fall. Her response touched him. Made her real. Vulnerable. Lured him in a way most women her age didn't because they were all about games and manipulation. "I always thought you and Granddad were happy together."

Nan pulled a tissue from the sleeve of her blouse and dabbed at her eyes. That done, she lifted her head and gave him a steady stare.

"Oh, Max. We were as happy as we could be with one another. My father… He caught me writing a letter to Aki after he was taken. He was horrified and told my mother I was to be married off as quickly as possible. He said it was to prevent the shame of my relationship with Aki from being known, but I knew it had far more to do with the business deal my father attempted to make with the Banes. I begged for news of Aki because my father had political connections in California. He refused to help me. But the next day, he came to me and said Aki had been killed in an accident at the camp not long after his arrival.

"I was so despondent I didn't care what happened to me after that. The marriage arrangements were made without my input. I stood there in silence while the justice married us. I don't believe I actually said 'I do,'" his grandmother said, her tone holding a puzzled note. "But it was done, and I started a new life with Leland."

Max met Holland's gaze, recognizing the softness in her eyes as a combination of pity and empathy and heartbreak for his grandmother.

"Max, it's no secret that your grandfather and I… struggled. He was photographed the world over with beautiful women, but we came from an era when divorce wasn't accepted like it is today."

"You wanted a divorce?" Max asked.

"No. At least, not at first. I tried, Max. Truly, I did. But when I found out about your grandfather's indiscretions, I thought of Aki and the love we shared. And I wondered… did my father lie about Aki's death?"

Nan turned her head to look at Holland. "Wouldn't you wonder, my dear? Do you think my daddy lied?"

Max watched as Holland struggled to form a response. She glanced at him, her teary gaze saying all the words she couldn't.

"I'm not… Oh, Violet, I don't know. Maybe… Maybe we could find out?"

"Could we?" Nan asked.

"What?" Max stared at Holland, unable to believe what he was hearing.

"It's a simple search. Maybe we could find records of Akihiro's presence in one of the camps? Or of the life he had afterward if…? There has to be records. The internet holds a lot of answers."

"You know how to do that, dear? Could you?"

"No. Nan… this is a bad idea. The letters were sweet but it's over. That life is over."

"Maximilian, I just want to know what happened to him."

"What good can come from it? And if the press somehow found out you were looking for some long-lost lover?"

"Max," Holland said, her tone shocked.

"No," he continued, ignoring all their looks and shocked expressions. "All of my life there has been one scandal after another. Why would you cause another one now?"

"It's a simple search," Holland said.

"I don't want her getting any more upset about this than she already is. We shouldn't have read the letters. Shouldn't have brought them to her attention," he said, shoving himself to his feet because he couldn't sit there with all three women looking at him like he was the one who'd imprisoned Akihiro all those years ago.

"Max, I may have forgotten where I hid the letters because of moving them so many times, but I've never forgotten them or Akihiro. After my father caught me writing to Aki, he searched my room from top to bottom and destroyed nearly all of them because I hadn't hidden them well enough. As soon as he left my room, I took the ones I had left and swore he'd never find them. Then I married, and I was terrified Leland would do the same. But you can't destroy love. Not when it's real. And nothing my father did or said ever changed how I felt about Aki."

Max stalked across the room to stand at the windows. He stared out at the water, wishing he was on a boat floating somewhere out there where scandals and secrets and greed weren't a reality. "Nan, you were teenagers. What you felt—both of you— it was more than likely hormones."

"Said like a man who has never been in love," Nan said, her tone thick with accusation and far too much awareness. "I know the difference between love and infatuation, Maximilian. And after all of these years, I want to know what happened. I *have* to know. That's actually the reason I hired Holland. Your father and uncle control my estate and would never condone my hiring someone to search for the truth. The money from the silver—gifts your cheating grandfather bought from his mistress to aid her life in Paris and brought home to me so I could be *thankful* for them, will go far to pay the fees."

"You can't be serious. That's what all of this is about?"

Nan lifted her chin, staring at him as only a woman with her age and wealth and determination could.

"It is. And until such time as I can afford to hire that professional, Holland can help me. She knows what it is like to lose the man she loved. You'll help me, won't you, my dear?"

Max turned in time to see Holland split her attention between his grandmother and him, and Max silently willed Holland to refuse.

"I-I… I'll do what I can."

"Thank you, Holland. Max? You'll help her?"

Max bit back the comment he wanted to say and settled for a hard twist of his head. "No way. You're on your own with this," he said as he stalked out of the room.

Minutes later he stood in his grandfather's study staring unseeingly at the contract he'd brought home with him earlier from the last round of negotiations, aware of the exact moment Holland entered.

What was it about her? Available and some not-so-available women tended to throw themselves when the Bane name was involved, but Holland wasn't throwing herself at him. If anything, it was the opposite. Especially since she'd agreed to the very thing he didn't want her to do.

"You hurt her, you know. Walking out like that."

He grimaced at the guilt he felt because he'd seen his grandmother's face as he'd left the room and knew Holland was right. "Giving her those letters was a mistake."

"How can you say that? Did you see her face when she realized what they were? Her reaction? Besides, from the sound of it, she'd already made her up mind to search for him and come up with a plan to make it happen."

Maybe that was true, but finding the letters had definitely added another layer of incentive where his grandmother was concerned. Then there was the debate of whether or not to inform his father and uncle. What would they say if they knew of their mother's plans?

Holland gripped his arm, urging him to face her. She stared up at him with her soulful brown eyes, her gaze searching his face.

He did his own bit of looking, learning the feminine angles and planes. The curve of her lips and cheekbones. Her features weren't perfect by society's standards, but to him they formed a face and a body that called to him as a man. "What good can come of finding him?"

"Everything."

"I don't agree."

"Max, you do remember that you're the one who wanted to take the letters to Violet, right?"

She had to point that out? "Regrettably."

"No, no regrets. Did you see her? She lit up the room when she talked about him. That kind of love is priceless."

"All the more reason to protect her from getting hurt again. At least now she can believe he's alive or dead or whatever she wants to believe, but once she knows for sure one way or the other, what then?"

"Then she gets closure. Max, *what if* her father lied to get her to submit to his wishes? *What if* Akihiro is alive and we can find him for her?"

"To what end? They're in their nineties, for God's sake."

"Oh, please. Your grandmother may be ninety-four but she's sharp as a tack and you know it. Max, they were in love. Surely that means something?"

"They had raging teenage hormones."

"Teenage hormones don't last seventy-nine *years*. It was real. The kind of love that *everyone* hopes to find but so few do."

"You did, from what Nan said. Can't be that unique."

She flinched at his comment and the sight made him regret the pettiness of his words. "I'm sorry. I shouldn't have said that."

"No, you shouldn't have. But she is right about one thing. I understand why this is so important to her. If

Akihiro is alive, how can you deny her what may be her last chance to see him? To stare into his eyes and just… love… one last time?"

"And if there is a Mrs. Tadashi?"

"Well, like you said, they're in their nineties."

Max lifted his hand and ran it roughly over his face, surrounded by the scent of a woman he barely knew and yet felt oddly connected to. Would he be as fascinated by Holland in seventy-nine years? Or would she be a memory of someone he once knew? When he was Nan's age, would he think the same of Holland?

"Max, it's just an internet search. You can think about it over dinner."

Dinner. A wry smile formed. "You're trying to distract me and bring me over to your way of thinking. It's a good negotiation tactic."

"Will it work?"

He lifted his hand and brushed a tendril of hair behind her ear, using the opportunity to run his knuckles over her soft cheek. "Depends on how well you negotiate over dinner."

Chapter 6

Holland excused herself to get ready for their dinner. He wanted to go to her favorite place so… that's exactly where they'd go.

Would he hate it?

She paused on her way to the closet, wondering if she needed to take a few minutes to finally do that internet search on Max. But it wasn't like a search would tell her what she wanted to know about him. Like what was his family like? Did he have siblings? They'd talked about her family during breakfast but the conversation was decidedly one-sided.

She continued on to the closet, feeling like Goldilocks when she perused the clothing she'd packed. Too little? Too much? What would be just right to wear to dinner with a billionaire currently angry with her for siding with his grandmother's plan to find her lost love? Would she be able to convince Max that helping Violet was simply the right thing to do?

Depends on how well you negotiate over dinner.

A shiver coursed through her at the memory of his

words and the look in his dark green gaze as he'd stared down at her. Her instincts told her she wasn't the only one intrigued.

She settled on a pair of gray skinny jeans that hugged her hips, low-heeled black booties, and an off-white blouse that brought out her eyes. On top of that, she'd add a black leather jacket to ward off the nighttime chill.

Her phone chimed and she glanced at the screen, shaking her head as she always did because Ireland seemed to have some sort of sixth sense when it came to her personal life.

Hey. News from you?

Found a secret compartment in the desk that's being donated to the auction so my mystery-solving alter ego got to play Nancy Drew.

Fun! Are you staying in? Dom is in Atlanta and I'm feeling lonely.

Yeah. Sorry. Londy or Frankie?

Busy. Sigh. Guess it's me and a movie.

Holland lifted her thumbs, wanting so badly to confide in Ireland about her dinner plans but knowing she shouldn't or else she'd risk a slew of more questions. *Enjoy,* she typed before setting the phone aside to finish her makeup.

Ireland's text had been a nice distraction from the nerves beginning to creep up, and once she finished her makeup, she donned the jacket and grabbed her phone and purse before heading toward the door.

She was a smart, capable, attractive woman. Dinner with a gorgeous billionaire? Pfffft. She had this.

Holland left her bedroom and moved down the hallway toward the stairs when a door opened down the hall. Max emerged, looking handsome as ever in dark-washed jeans and a dark burgundy pullover. He carried his jacket in his hand and paused when he spotted her, his gaze sweeping over her from head to booties and back up again. *Lingering*.

"You look beautiful."

"Thank you. Are you ready to go?"

"Yeah. But I'll need directions or an address."

She shook her head. "I'll drive us."

Max's gaze narrowed on her and she shrugged. "I lost the bet. I know the way. Why not?"

"Why not, indeed? After you."

THE LIGHT SCENT of Holland's perfume teased Max's senses during the walk down the stairs to the lower level. He wasn't normally fond of perfumes but Holland's was light and airy, there but not.

"Does the thought of me driving make you nervous?"

Max lowered his head a bit and smiled. "No. Though it feels ungentlemanly for some reason."

"Ah, and here I thought you were a modern man."

"Apparently I have some old-fashioned qualities left. So, where are we going?"

"Mm. You'll see."

Max walked Holland past the SUV he'd rented for his stay and opened the door of her gray Audi for her to climb behind the wheel.

"What kind of music do you like?" she asked once he was inside.

"Depends on my mood."

"And your mood tonight?"

She smiled at him from across the vehicle, and he fought off the urge to lean toward her and see if she'd let him kiss her. "Surprise me. Maybe it'll match where we're going for dinner."

She laughed and found a station on the satellite radio

and saxophone music filled the space, low enough to still hold a conversation. Maybe dinner at a jazz place?

"So what do you do when you're not working or traveling?" he asked.

"Books. I love reading."

"What kind of books?"

A flush of color began filling her cheeks and his interest soared.

"Uh, lots of things but mostly… romance novels."

"Those books with the men on the covers that apparently don't own shirts?"

She wrinkled her nose but nodded as she made the turns leading out of the private, gated area where his grandmother's house was located and got them onto the main road leading into Wilmington.

"Those are the ones. While my peers read blogs and self-help and books about taking control of one's life, I love reading… about love."

"You mean sex."

"Nooo," she countered with a shake of her head and a glance across the interior. "Love. Two people, problems, and the way they overcome them. They're not all about sex. Some don't have any sex in them at all. What?" she asked, a laugh bubbling out of her. "You asked and I'm being honest."

"I thought by the blush you were going to say you had a secret life or something."

"Well, I kind of do. I have a secret name online. As a reviewer."

"A reviewer?"

"Yeah. And, no, I'm not going to tell you what it is. That will require a rematch at billiards, thank you."

"Consider it done. Why romance?"

"Isn't everyone searching for love? Wanting to be loved?"

He was very well aware of the heightened tension after her question. "You're referring to my grandmother."

"Well, yeah. Violet's story, the letters, all of it… Not to bring up a touchy subject, but it's really got me thinking about life and… stuff. She has every right to want to know the truth of what happened."

"I don't suppose you'd fill me in on the love you lost? Or is that too painful a topic?"

"It's… complicated. He was amazing. Driven. Special Forces," she said, sliding a glance in Max's direction. "He wanted more, but something always held me back."

"What happened?"

"He popped the question, I said no, he returned to duty and… soon after, like really soon after, he was killed."

"You feel responsible."

"Wouldn't you? He loved me. I know he loved me and I loved him but… not enough. I hurt him, and I wonder if his head was where it needed to be when it happened."

"What does your family say?"

He watched as she inhaled and flashed a shaky smile. "That I did the right thing and he did what he was called to do."

"You don't believe them?"

She was silent a long moment, the music filling the air covering the silence.

"I'm honestly not sure. I hope it's true."

She slid another look across the expanse of the interior.

"Was Violet right? When she said you've never been in love?"

He smoothed the edge of his thumb over the top of his jeans as he stared out at the passing scenery. "I was engaged once. Briefly. Nan doesn't know. No one in my family knew. It was over before it started."

"Are you really going to make me ask?"

He chuckled softly and shifted in the seat toward her, liking the confident way she drove and the way she looked behind the wheel of the low-slung vehicle. "It's complicated," he said, repeating her words. Because how did a man with the money he had say he wanted to be loved for himself without coming off like a whining loser?

"You're not going to tell on your grandmother, are you? What she plans? I mean, I get it if you do but... is she right? Would your father and uncle try to keep her from finding Akihiro?"

"Probably. My uncle and aunt are overseas. Missionaries. Uncle Jack would be concerned but probably not an issue. My parents... That's another story."

"But why? I'm sorry, maybe it's a stupid question to you, but why would they keep her from finding the man she once loved so very much?"

"It's difficult to answer that because of the many aspects involved."

"You're worried Akihiro or his family might try to take advantage?"

"Yes. Of course. My grandmother is an extremely wealthy woman. But there's the social aspect as well."

"By social you mean scandal? Are you really worried so much about what strangers think?"

When she put it that way... "Holland, I don't want her getting hurt. Period."

"Okay, I accept that. But I also say not letting her have closure hurts her so... it's a pick-your-poison kind of thing, in my opinion."

"Perhaps."

"What about your parents? We talked about my family

over breakfast but you didn't say much about yours. Are they divorced? Together?"

"Together. Living separately most of the time and… going through the motions."

She slowly stopped at a red light but didn't take her gaze from the traffic in front of her.

"That's sad. I mean, all couples go through stages of growth and change but… I wouldn't be happy with that. Touchy subject or not, you should give your grandmother full credit for being a classy woman for all of those years with your grandfather."

He inhaled and sighed. "Agreed. But I'm struggling to see how this is date conversation."

"Are we on a date? Because I thought I was just paying a bet."

He laughed at her blunt response. "I guess that means I'll have to take you on a real one so you can tell the difference."

Once again her face flooded with color and the awareness of her response heated his blood. "And I'll take that blush as a yes. Be honest. Did you research me the way you do your listings?"

"Yes and no. I looked Violet up and read about her charitable work along with your grandfather's business dealings over the years after she contacted me, but I haven't had time to research you specifically. Plus, I'd much rather get my information from the source."

"Would you now? What would you like to know?"

"Oh, I don't know. Where's home? Do you have siblings? Who's your favorite sports team?"

He liked the lightened tone of her questions after the heaviness of before. "I have a few places I call home. In the States, it's New York. One brother, JC, also in business, and a younger sister, Sophia, who married last year. As to sports teams… the Yankees."

"Good team."

"Great team."

"What's Christmas like with your family?"

"Chaotic. There's inevitably talk of business and politics and then lots of yelling."

Another low, sultry laugh. It teased his senses and made him want to hear more.

"Do you see your family often?"

"Once or twice a year. I try to schedule any out-of-New-York meetings for this area when I can so that I can see Nan, but on holidays, those who can make it show up at my parents' home in Virginia."

"Violet mentioned living in Virginia in passing. How did she wind up here?"

"It was their summer home, purchased to be close to Uncle Jack when he and his wife led a church here. This house was the one Nan always favored, though."

Holland continued to drive them toward their destination as they got to know one another. They left the subject of family and went on to movies and music and things to do in the area.

She made a few turns and signaled to pull into a parking lot of a seemingly residential area.

"Hope you're hungry."

"I am, but… Are you sure we're in the right place?" It looked familiar. Very familiar, actually.

Holland grinned at him and unbuckled her seat belt. "You'll see."

Once more he rounded the vehicle to hold her door while she emerged. The breeze brought her scent to his nose and he inhaled appreciatively. "That's nice. Your perfume."

"Thank you. I found it in a little shop in Belgium."

"How often do you travel?"

"Often enough for the novelty to have worn off. I get tired of it sometimes," she said. "But I usually have just long enough of a break in between trips to reboot before going again."

She steered him down a sidewalk along the side of a church. "Are you leading me into a dark alley?"

Her laugh filled his ears.

"Scared I won't protect you?"

"Come on, where are we going?"

"My favorite place to eat."

"Which is?"

"Nairobi."

"What?"

She hurried the last several steps to an unmarked door and grasped the handle, grinning at him.

"You said to bring you to my favorite place so... welcome to Africa."

Chapter 7

Max wasn't sure where they were going, only that Holland had either lied about researching him—which he didn't think she had— or her surprise was about to get even more interesting.

There were people in matching T-shirts acting as volunteers helping to distribute food and drinks and chatting up those who'd come to partake of the free food, but when Holland led him toward the kitchen area and a man spotted them, he left his post and came running.

"Hey! Rehema, come see who is visiting us!"

Max's hand fell from the base of her back as Holland stepped forward to hug the young man. While they greeted each other, Max remained a few steps behind amongst the crowd waiting patiently to get their food, trying to take it all in while wondering if God was up there in heaven chuckling. Timing was everything, wasn't it?

A beautiful young woman appeared from behind a door, smiling as she spotted her husband hugging Holland. She must have sensed his stare because her gaze shifted to him.

"Mr. Max!"

Max grinned and welcomed the woman with open arms. "Hello, Rehema. You look beautiful as always. How is Marcus treating you?"

"He is everything you said he was and more," Rehema stated.

Holland had turned at the sound of Rehema's greeting and now watched as he hugged the woman and kissed her on her cheek. "How's the baby?" he asked, refocusing his attention to his friend.

The woman smoothed her hands over her very pregnant belly and practically glowed with happiness.

"Getting too big to stay in much longer. And it's a boy!"

"That's wonderful news. Congratulations."

"Thank you."

Holland and Marcus joined them, and Max was very aware of Holland's wide-eyed curiosity.

Rehema nudged her husband. "Tell Mr. Max the name."

Max split his attention between the happy couple and Holland, amused by her speechlessness. He liked that her surprise had turned on her. "Tell me what?"

"Now that we know it's a boy, we'd like to name him Max," Marcus said. "In your honor for all you've done for us."

"Would that be all right with you?" Rehema asked, her beautiful brown eyes staring up at Max with expectation.

"The honor would be mine, Rehema."

"How do you know each other?" Holland asked, her voice filled with more than a little bemusement.

"Wait, you're here with Mr. Max?" Marcus's expression shifted into knowing awareness as he clapped Max on the shoulder. "Lucky man."

"I am," Max said, holding Holland's gaze.

"It's good to see you again, Ms. Holland. We've missed you," Rehema said, hugging Holland.

"And I have you, Rehema. And, please, it's Holland. But I'm still curious as to how you know Max?"

"And how you know Marcus and Rehema," Max added.

"For such a big world, it is very small, yes?" Marcus said. "We met Ms. Holland—Holland," Marcus corrected when he saw Holland opening her mouth to protest, "last year during the fundraiser. Now whenever she is in town during our Nairobi nights, she comes to eat with us."

"I see."

For the first time since they'd arrived, Max pondered the possibility that Holland had brought him here as some kind of test. He just wasn't sure why. Maybe to see if he'd run because they were in the church's soup kitchen? It wasn't exactly a normal first date. So if that was the case, what was the reason behind the test?

"Come. Sit. We have plenty of food."

The couple took them to a table and Max held Holland's chair for her before he joined her. Rehema and Marcus quickly filled plates for them and Rehema brought them to the table while Marcus went to get them drinks.

"Rehema, please, you don't have to wait on us," Holland said.

"I insist. It is because of you and Mr. Max that we are able to do this. To give back to the people who took us in when we were so desperate to escape. We wouldn't be here if not for you both. It's our pleasure."

The plates were filled with Rehema's fabulous cooking, a buffet of piri piri chicken, jollof rice, and bunny chow. The choices provided were no doubt intended to fill empty bellies, but it was a culinary delight Max had tasted before when visiting Uncle Jack six months ago.

The couple sat with them for a few minutes while they ate but then excused themselves to go back to the kitchen. Holland finished chewing and reached for her drink, all the while studying Max. "You have a question?" he asked.

"Just thinking."

"About?"

"You. Here I thought I'd managed to pull off one awesome surprise, but instead, you surprised me. That doesn't happen very often."

"Likewise. What? Did you think I'm too rich to eat with the homeless?"

"Maybe. I mean, I truly came to see Rehema and Marcus because this is my favorite place to eat on Nairobi nights, so it was just good timing, but…"

"But you wondered what kind of man I really am. Curiosity satisfied?"

She lowered her long lashes over her eyes, a tantalizing feminine smile curling her lips.

"Mmm. Not even close."

The comment seared Max's brain and sent his body into overdrive. After a long, heated moment when he didn't disguise his thoughts as he stared at her, he took a breath and forced himself to temper the desire to know all there was to know about Holland. *Patience.* "Well, in case you haven't noticed, I'm not running away from Rehema's delicious food."

"So I see. How did you meet them? Because I have a feeling it may be the more interesting story compared to my fundraiser one."

"Marcus saved my life a couple of years ago when I was in Africa working with my uncle, Jack. Marcus took a bullet intended for me. When I asked him what was the one thing he wanted more than anything else in the world, he said he wanted to be a US citizen. He and

Rehema were engaged at the time and he worried about her safety and that of their future family. The news here talks of shootings, but we have no idea what others live through on a daily basis in other parts of the world. Just trying to survive hour by hour. I went to work getting them visas."

"But you said you live in New York. How did they wind up here?"

Max's grin widened. "My uncle used to pastor this church and now it supports their mission work. I knew it looked familiar when you pulled in but I wasn't sure until I saw Marcus."

Holland lowered her head, her teeth sinking into her lip as she slowly shook her head back and forth.

"Small world," she said softly.

"The congregation was a support network they wouldn't have had in New York so… they chose to come here."

"That's a pretty cool gift to give someone."

"It was nothing compared to what Marcus did for me."

"Who was shooting at you?"

"Local drug lord. He didn't like it that I'd come to help the village. I became enemy number one."

"May I ask how you wound up over there? I mean, I get helping your uncle's work, but that's not the norm for most men in your financial position."

"Ah. That is a story to be told somewhere other than here," he murmured. "If you've finished, we can head out, though. So they don't feel they have to entertain us."

Holland turned to see the couple looking their way while trying to work the kitchen. "Good idea. I'll text Rehema later this week and invite her to Ireland's baby shower. We could turn it into a surprise for Rehema, too."

Holland stated the idea casually, like it was no big deal,

but he saw her heart behind it. "I'm sure she would love that."

Max and Holland said their goodbyes to Marcus and Rehema before walking toward the exit. Along the way, Max got waylaid by several of the church officials who helped keep the soup kitchen going. While he chatted with them, he watched as Holland moved closer to a door leading into the church instead of their exit. And even though she was discreet and he nearly missed the slip of her hand over the donation box, he knew then what she'd done. This program was important. The crowd gathered was proof.

Holland had moved to a painting along the wall when Max joined her. "I saw that."

"What?"

He narrowed his gaze on her beautiful face but he didn't comment further. She stared up at him, the height difference bringing her head to shoulder level.

"Ready?"

"Lead the way." When she turned toward the exit, a few strands of her hair caught in the whiskers on his chin, entangling them for a split second. Holland froze, wide-eyed and lips parted, as he gently smoothed her hair back into place. He ran his knuckles over her cheek to her chin, lifting it higher, while reminding himself that a church annex wasn't an appropriate location for their first kiss. After a long moment, he stepped back and gently slid the hand to her shoulder and around her back instead. "Where to now?"

"Dancing?"

A low chuckle rumbled out of his chest. "No. Somewhere quiet."

MAX WALKED her to her Audi and tucked her behind the wheel. She watched as he rounded the front of her car, using the moment alone to attempt to regain her equilibrium. Max was a lot to take in. More than looks, more than money. Just… more.

Once he climbed in beside her and fastened his seat belt, she got them moving. "Would you like a coffee? Maybe some tea? There's a coffee shop down by the river."

"That sounds good."

She drove several miles toward the river walk before pulling off into the parking area of the trendy coffee shop. "Whatever you do, if you meet my sister London, don't tell her I brought you here."

Max chuckled and held the door for her. Once they had their orders, they moved to a set of empty chairs. She turned toward him, wondering when she'd hit the age of liking a man for who he wasn't rather than who he was. "The church is doing good work there. Rehema has mentioned it quite a few times in passing when we've discussed the food for the upcoming fundraiser."

"Is it related to the auction Nan donated the desk to?"

"Yeah. The proceeds help the city shelters and homeless population."

Max gave her a long stare.

"You make me nervous when you do that," she admitted. "It's like you're dissecting me. Or trying to."

"My apologies. My intention isn't to make you uncomfortable."

"So what is the intention then?"

"To get to know you. We might disagree on whether or not Nan should delve into the past, but I am drawn to you, Holland. The problem is that I won't be in town long. Once my business is concluded, I'll return to South Africa."

"Wait. Return?"

"One of my other homes."

"You mentioned helping your uncle earlier. Now you say you live there."

"It's a second home to me. Has been since college. And if you're wondering if there is a special someone there, no. It's… a lot of someones."

"People you help."

"Yes. The start-ups fund much of the work I do alongside my aunt and uncle."

"I see. So my next question is what leads a man like you to do such a thing? I'm guessing if you chose to, you'd never have to work another day in your life. So what drives you?"

"I could say it's just a characteristic of mine."

"Is it?"

"Not entirely. I hated it when I was first sent to stay with my uncle. It was… a punishment. A way of getting me out of the States and away from the media."

Oh, whatever was that about? "And you needed to be away from it because…?"

Once more that forest-green gaze narrowed on her and sucked the air from her lungs.

"You really don't know?"

"I wouldn't ask if I did."

Silence. Long, uncomfortable seconds ticked by as they maintained eye contact, frozen.

"I killed my best friend."

Holland blinked, sure her expression revealed her shock at his words no matter how hard she tried to school her features, but of all things he could've said, that wasn't what she expected. "Pardon?"

"Alec. We were college freshmen on spring break. Too

stupid and too rich to have a care or thought of consequences."

She forced herself to take a sip of her decaf latte but she might as well have been drinking mud for all the flavor it held after hearing his confession. "What happened?"

She'd worked her job long enough to have witnessed some pretty dark family secrets. She'd even been on the receiving end of proposals and propositions that would make a high-end call girl blush. Nasty people were just nasty people but rich nasty people were cut from a different cloth. Entitled. Self-centered. They didn't possess empathy or concern for anything other than themselves and their desires. Get in their way, make them angry, and nothing was off-limits. But nothing about Max equalled that. Was she missing something?

"We partied. Drank enough for a frat house, let alone two pathetic frat boys, and then had the bright idea to go swimming."

Her stomach sank like a weight. The comment he'd made to her about no longer swimming came to mind. Apparently this was where it originated. The why of why he didn't.

"The girls we're with tell us to race, see who is the better man. So we go in and we're laughing and dunking each other. Everything is fine. Then we take off and when I get to the other side I realize Alec isn't anywhere close. So I go back in, call for him, look for him, dive. He was gone. The girls… they didn't even notice he'd gone under. Alec had passed out from all the alcohol and drowned, and none of us noticed. *I* didn't notice," Max said. "I wasn't such a good friend."

"Max… I'm so sorry." There was nothing more she could say. Not when she could read his expression and knew nothing would ever change the way he felt about what happened. He blamed himself, and she knew, in his position, she probably would, too. "That's a horrible thing to happen, a tragedy, but unless you forced him into the water and then held him under, you realize you're not to blame. Right?"

Max didn't respond to her question. He stared at his coffee cup. Fumbled with the sleeve on the bottom. It took him a long while before he met her gaze again. "Due to my family name, the media swarmed. It was crazy. All of it. My father sent me to his brother, the one member of the family referred to as the 'saint' because he'd become a minister early on. He worked in Haiti then. When I got there and managed to pull my head out of my rear, I realized how blessed a life I had. And how, if I concentrated on the work, I found relief from the pain I felt due to Alec's death."

"Hard work is good for that."

He stretched out his fingers before curling them around his cup once more.

"It was a lifesaver for me. But the summer ended and I went back to school, and life—I—was never the same. Every break after that, I went to stay with my uncle and aunt wherever they were, and I realized more than anything, the main thing they needed was funding."

"That's why you focus so heavily on start-ups?"

He nodded. "I'm good at it. And it gives me the flexibility and financial security I need to be where I want to be."

"Hands on," she murmured. "That's quite a story that brought you to where you are now."

"It won't bring Alec back."

"No. But look at what it's propelled you to do. My sister —London—has this mantra about learning to love fast because we never know what time we'll have with someone.

We all learned it because of moving around in the military so much, but London has always keenly focused on loving whoever appears in her life while she's able, as long as she's able. I think it fits here, as well."

"You're telling me you love me?"

His expression made her laugh and earned her looks from the others in the building. "I'm *saying* you loved Alec for as long as he was your friend, and when he passed, you carried that love into what you're doing now. You used it for something better rather than letting it destroy you. Max, you're honoring his memory and that means something. Don't you think?"

Max leaned toward her and she wished they'd chosen to sit on one of the empty couches rather than the chairs. Maybe if they'd been on the couch, he'd use the moment to move closer and cuddle her to his side. As it was, he reached out and grasped her hand in his, squeezed her fingers. And made her happy she hadn't found out about his past from the internet. That bit of his life needed to be told in person by the person who'd lived it rather than a media frenzy looking to sell stories by making up things about a heartbroken young man in mourning. "Max, I'm sorry you lost your friend. But I'm glad you shared that with me."

He lifted her fingers to his lips and kissed them. "You made it easy."

"Good."

He smiled at her. Held her gaze for a long, breath-stealing moment. "Now, Holland Cohen, it's time."

"Oh? For what?"

"For you to tell me your biggest, deepest, darkest secret."

Chapter 8

Max watched as Holland's expression changed, but he couldn't quite pin down the flashes moving so rapidly across her face. "Was that a tough request?"

"No," she said with an uncomfortable-sounding laugh. "It's just difficult to answer."

"Because you have so many deep, dark secrets?" His mind immediately went to an unflattering place before he reeled it in and forced himself to focus.

"Because my answers will reveal more than you probably want to know."

He set the coffee cup aside and leaned toward her. "You can't say that and not follow it up, you know."

She laughed at his statement but the sound was full of embarrassment and hesitation.

"Hey, I told you mine. And it was a doozy."

"So I have to share? Fine. I… have a problem no one knows about."

"Involving?"

"Speed. If I get another ticket, I have to go see the judge and will probably be assigned community service."

Max stared at her, struggling to conceal his amusement. "Trying out for Daytona?"

"Something like that, yeah."

"I'm almost afraid to ask about your other secrets."

"They're bad, too," she said, her tone apologetic.

"Go on."

"Well, I hate ice cream. And apple pie. I know it's weird and un-American, but it's true. I'm also terrified of snakes. Like hard-core terrified because if I'd ever see one in a house, it would have to be burned down, no question."

"I see. Is that it?"

"Talk radio. Hate it. Who wants to listen to people argue over everything? Give me music or news but don't torture me by forcing me to listen to that garbage. If I want to fight, I'll pick one with one of my sisters."

Max stared at Holland and wondered if it was possible to fall in love in such a short amount of time. She was attractive. Beautiful. But it was her quick wit and humor that drew him. And just because he also liked the thrill of speed, he'd love to surprise her with a trip to a race track and turn her loose.

The warmth and friendship Holland had shown Rehema and Marcus, the way she treated his grandmother... Her integrity was something to be valued beyond measure.

Holland inhaled and exhaled with a low sigh.

"Wow. Confession is good for the soul. I feel better."

He laughed and shook his head. The last time he was out with a woman, she'd spent the entire time gossiping about people who were supposedly good friends. But tonight he'd spent most of the evening laughing and wondering if it was possible to truly know a woman like Holland completely.

"Would you like to walk along the river?"

"Let's go."

They threw away their cups and moved toward the door. Holland paused to zip her coat, and he stepped forward to help, using it as an excuse to touch her. That done, he slid his hands around the collar to gather her long hair, liking the silken length as it slid through his fingers.

"Thank you."

"You're welcome." He stared down at her, imprinting her appearance on his mind as he pondered her secrets. If those were the worst she could come up with, she lived an honest life. Something else to admire. Because if she was reading all of those books and posting reviews, odds were she wasn't in a hotel bar trying to hook up with strangers just because.

The river walk was just outside the doors of the coffee shop and they headed toward the long planks in silence. Along the way, Max draped his arm over Holland's shoulders and tugged her close, tucking her against his side and noting the fact she curled against him, slipping her arm around his waist beneath his jacket.

They strolled along the boardwalk and enjoyed the peacefulness of the evening. After a while, they paused, and Holland stared up at him, her eyes glistening from the lights positioned periodically along the way.

"Have you ever been to Africa?" The question came out of nowhere and yet, once voiced, he didn't regret it.

"No."

"Would you like to see it?"

"Mmm. I will admit to wondering if I should stop by to see you in action the next time I'm on that side of the world."

He moved closer, lifted his hands to snag her collar and tug it higher to protect her from the cool breeze. He didn't let go, though, and used his hold to tug her another step closer while lowering his head.

The last woman he'd dated had demanded he stop his nonsense about giving his money away and grow up. Holland wanted to come see it, and after tonight, he knew she'd be the type to get her hands dirty, too. "You could stop by. Or you could plan a visit, stay a while, and really see what it's about."

It was a challenge and a request in one. And he couldn't wait to see if she made an excuse or stepped up.

"Is that an invitation?"

He lowered his head even more and brushed his lips over hers, holding her gaze and watching as her eyes softened. Her breath hitched in her chest and he pressed harder, deepening the kiss and wrapping her in his arms, learning the feel and taste of her, her scent swirling in his senses until he felt drunk on it and wanted more.

He guided her backward until her hips rested against the beams lining the walk and supported her. Then he took the kisses deeper still, not stopping until she gripped his arms and a soft sound emerged from her throat that singed his blood and set him on fire.

The sound of a group of people walking by alerted him to their lack of privacy. Max ended the kiss and lifted his head but stayed positioned where he was, her heavy-lidded gaze and full lips holding his undivided attention. "I asked for dancing but I'd rather kiss you again."

A nod was her answer.

"Holland?"

"Mmm?"

He brushed another kiss across her lips, deciding the lack of privacy was a good thing since it would keep him in check but allow him to kiss her as he pleased. "It was definitely an invitation."

MAX TOOK Holland out again the following evening. Now she sat across the table from him at a nice restaurant, aware of more than one envious female glance piercing them from the bar area. Had she not felt fairly confident in herself, she would've been hard-pressed not to squirm from her feelings of inadequacy.

Too much time sitting in airports and writing descriptions of the items she'd researched and photographed, not to mention her love of reading, meant a constant battle with weight due to the heavenly tastes of the food from around the world. Max didn't seem to mind her curves, though. Not when he looked at her the way that he did. "Have I mentioned how good you look in leather?"

Her words brought a sexy tilt to his lips.

"I think I should be the one giving you compliments. That dress," he said, his gaze lowering to what he could see of her above the table, "is amazing. You look amazing. Which is why I'm sitting here wondering why you want to talk about my grandmother's dating life instead of ours."

He pierced her with his gaze, and it was a struggle for her to regulate her breathing, especially after that dating comment.

"Holland, why is finding Akihiro Tadashi so important to you? Because you feel my grandmother settled?"

Settled? Oh, touchy ground. Max was a Bane male with a heavy sense of pride. *Tread carefully*, her mind warned. "I think you read the letters the same as I did. She didn't have a choice, Max. It was a different world then, and she did what her family expected of her, partly because she was so heartbroken. But even though it may not have been her choice at the time, I have never heard a woman say she's regretted her children and *grand*children.

She loves you, Max. You know she doesn't regret anything to do with having you."

Max pondered her words for a quiet moment before reaching out to lift his glass from the table.

"Well, we can't change the past but here's to not settling."

She smiled at him and clinked her glass to his. "To not settling."

While she sipped her drink and held Max's gaze, a waiter arrived with their food order. Dinner conversation ranged from their travel experiences and bad airport food to Max's plans to help his uncle build a school in Africa. "You really love it there, don't you?"

"Sorry. I'm going on about it too much."

"No, not at all. You're very passionate about the work you're doing and for good reason. Will you continue to focus your time in Africa or move on to other countries?"

"That's a good question. There are plenty of places in need, so I'm sure the work will travel to a new location at some point. I'm not sure when, though."

"You know, there aren't a lot of men in your position willing to give the majority of their hard work away."

"I have more than enough to keep me and my future family fed in my old age," he said.

Holland frowned at his tone, sensing that she'd hit a nerve but unsure of why. "It's a calling you feel, isn't it? Don't apologize for that," she said before he could answer. "Everyone should be so blessed that they get to do what they love in life."

She noted that, with her statement, the tension that had appeared so suddenly eased.

"What about you? Do you love what you do?"

Another tough question. One she'd been pondering a lot lately. "I love certain aspects of it. The travel, for sure.

Being able to see places I'd probably never get to go to working a regular job. But it has its downsides, too. I wind up with families who have overextended and selling the items is a sad attempt to recoup money or a last-ditch effort to avoid foreclosure and public shame. They don't say so while hiring the company I work for, of course, but when I'm in their home, I inevitably hear things. The upside to that, however, is that the items go to another home and aren't wasted, and the money helps, for a while at least. But living out of a suitcase gets old, as does getting stuck in airports."

"And your future? What does it look like?"

"Oh, who knows the answer to that? The future will play out as it's meant to. And I'm okay with that," she said, lifting her shoulders in a shrug. "I think when the time is right for me to make a change, I'll know."

"You trust your gut instinct. That's good. That's a trait some people struggle with their entire lives."

A long silence fell over the table as they stared into each other's eyes. Her pulse picked up speed at what she thought she saw.

Max sat forward in his chair.

"Did you, uh, find any information today during your search for Akihiro?"

Now who was the one wanting to talk about his grandmother's boyfriend? "Tadashi is a popular last name. Thankfully there were a limited number of camps in California. Still, most of the records only show a first initial, so that has definitely slowed me down."

"Maybe it's for the best."

The best for whom? "I'm sorry this is so hard for you, Max."

"It's an adjustment in thinking, for sure. My grandfather could have been a better husband. I know that. There have always been whispers amongst the staff, gossip at parties. Even a few irate husbands cornering my grandfather from time to time. I may have been young, but it wasn't long before I knew what everyone meant when they talked about his indiscretions. Has Sally told you yet? About the reason behind the insane amount of silver Nan is having you list?"

Holland sucked in a sharp breath.

"Yeah. With every trip he'd bring Nan a gift more elaborate than the last. The family used to comment on it, how sweet it was, how much he treasured her, but I overheard my grandfather talking to my father about how his Paris mistress picked out Nan's gifts. The woman worked at the business and of course earned a commission for the sales."

Holland closed her eyes briefly. "What a thing for a kid to overhear. That's horrible."

"I never looked at my grandfather the same after that. I could never treat my wife that way. Marriage is meant to be honored. Respected. The saying that the grass is greener is ridiculous because it's greener where you water it."

Not long after Max uttered those words, he said her name.

"I said we'd go dancing and we didn't. Would you like to?"

He tilted his head toward the opposite side of the room and she accepted the invitation with a ready nod. "Love to."

Max held her hand as he guided her onto the dance floor. He took her into his arms, held her against his strength, and she reveled in the feel of whatever it was happening between them. Too fast. Too risky. But real?

They danced for several songs. He held her hand to his chest, his other hand at the small of her back, searing her.

His lips brushed against her temple from time to time, and she turned her face into his jawline and closed her eyes.

Was it wrong for her to want his business in town to drag on as long as possible so this didn't end?

"What are you thinking?"

She tilted her head back, nuzzling his strong jaw in the process. "Wishing I could freeze time."

His fingers tightened at her waist, on the hand he held to his chest.

"Me, too."

But as they moved and swayed to the music, time ticked on and the night grew darker outside the oceanfront windows.

"Ready to head back?"

Back. Not home. Because this wasn't Max's home. It was barely hers as much as she traveled. Neither of them really had a place to land. Called somewhere home. "Whenever you are."

They were making their way to the door when someone called Holland's name. She turned to find Ireland and Dominic walking toward them at a brisk pace.

"Sister?"

Max breathed the word close to her ear and she shivered even as she nodded.

"You resemble each other."

"Hi," Ireland said, smiling at Holland and giving her a brief hug before turning her full attention to Max. "Who's this?"

"Uhh…"

"Maximilian Bane."

Holland saw the slight widening of Ireland's eyes when Max's name registered.

"Dominic and Ireland Sage. Pleasure," Dominic said, shaking Max's hand.

"You two looked like you were having fun on the dance floor," Ireland said.

"We were," Holland said, giving her sister a pointed glare to mind her questions. And her manners. "But we were just leaving."

"Oh. I'd hoped you'd join us for dessert."

Max looked at her as though leaving the decision in her hands but Holland quickly shook her head. "I'm sorry. We have to go."

"Another time," Max stated politely.

Ireland reluctantly said goodbye and Holland knew she would pay for the quick exit later.

Outside the restaurant, Max handed the ticket to the valet and they waited for the twentysomething to bring the SUV.

"Is there a particular reason you forgot my name and didn't want to join them?"

She hugged her arms around her front and pinned a smile to her lips. "Just trying to avoid sisterly intrusion."

Max's gaze narrowed on her as though he didn't believe the excuse, but she wasn't able to form a better one. Lying was never her thing, and truth was, she'd wanted to join them, to sit across the table from them and laugh and talk and be a couple, out with another couple.

But they weren't. And who knew if they ever could be given their complicated lives. Wishes and wants weren't reality. And Max's identity, his very being, was a complication all on its own.

Max drove them back to Violet's and she wondered if this was what it would be like as a couple. This quiet moment. Dinner dates and the like. Was it possible with their lifestyles? Her job? His work both in business and with his charities? Or was she dreaming of the old-fashioned kind of lost love that was no longer found? The kind depicted in old movies that people today thought so unrealistic.

Max walked her to her bedroom door and left her with another set of breath-stealing kisses that rocked her world and made her dream of impossible things. Then he walked away and she wondered—too late—if it was wise to get as involved as she was because it meant watching him walk away a lot.

Was she really falling for a man who traveled to dangerous areas, who was periodically shot at because of drug lords? Where men like Max were kidnapped and ransomed? The places that needed help most, the places Max liked to go, weren't safe. Could she live with that?

What happened to loving fast? Living life a moment at a time?

Holland entered her bedroom and changed into a sleep shirt before grabbing her phone. Normally the sister version of a 911 call meant meeting with all four of them at the dream catcher mailbox to discuss whatever was on their minds, but given the distance and time of night and the fact she wanted to keep her private life as private as possible, she had to settle for a text.

I'm sorry we didn't stay and have dessert.

Maximilian Bane??? Ireland texted.

I know. Trust me. I do. Just… tell me no.

If you know it's probably a bad idea, why do you need to hear it?

Holland closed her eyes and tried to find the words. *Because I'm falling hard.*

FAST.

And his life is way more complicated than mine. It's doomed. Why am I doing this to myself?

He must be something special if that's the case.

Or maybe I'm just setting myself up to fail with a man who isn't like his peers?

Holl, falling in love isn't failing.

It is when you know it'll end in a broken heart.

Does it have to? Are you seeing red flags or panicking over something that hasn't happened yet?

He spends most of his time in Africa helping those who need it most. It's dangerous, it's scary. It's admirable and unselfish and heroic and sexy as all get out. But to be with him...

Silence. Holland could almost see Ireland's puckered eyebrows as she pondered the text Holland had sent. Holland waited. And waited. Finally the little dots indicating Ireland typed appeared.

We love who we love. Be present NOW. Enjoy NOW. Don't worry about tomorrow. You can't do more than that.

Holland stared at the phone. Violet's sweet young romance was proof of those very statements. Who knew what tomorrow would bring?

Who knew what would happen next?

Chapter 9

Several days later, Max sat in the second-floor living room with his grandmother while waiting on Holland to appear for their evening out. While Holland spent her days photographing and researching and writing the descriptions for the many pieces of silver and items his grandmother wanted to consign, she spent her evenings with him. They'd gone out to dinners, taken a walk on the beach and had a picnic, and perused an art museum. But he was all too aware of the fact Holland had started avoiding the subject of his grandmother's request to search for Akihiro because they couldn't come to terms.

Nan sipped a cup of herbal tea and stared at him over the rim of the delicate cup.

"You're frowning, dear, and looking quite fierce. What are you pondering so? Your business dealings?"

He inhaled and sat forward in the chair, elbows to knees and hands clasped in front of him while he broached the touchy subject he'd avoided for far too long. "Nan, I want to ask you something and I want you to tell me the truth. Are you okay?"

"What do you mean, dear?"

"Are you having health issues? Are you worried about something financial?" he asked. "Is there a reason you've decided to hire Holland's company and pursue this thing with Akihiro that you haven't shared?"

"Oh, Max. I am perfectly fine. For all his faults, your grandfather provided well for me. And I don't have any medical issue beyond what anyone my age has. But these things," she said, lifting a hand toward the dining area where Sally sat polishing the silver Holland had yet to photograph, "they're ugly to me and they make me sad. I should've gotten rid of them long ago, and I love the idea of using the money to find my first love. It seems… fitting. I know you don't agree but that's how I feel. Even if it makes you uncomfortable."

He nodded slowly and reached out to lightly squeeze her knee. "I may not agree, but I love you."

"I love you, too, my dear boy. Now, what are your plans for Holland this evening?"

Max met his grandmother's too-knowing gaze and grinned. "It's a surprise. Something I hope she will enjoy."

"Hmm. You're spending a lot of time together. And don't think my old eyes haven't caught the looks you two exchange."

Max leaned back in the chair and waited for his grandmother to continue. "She's… different. Special."

"That she is. I'm glad you see it as well. Holland is very grounded, isn't she? Down-to-earth. She isn't a spoiled socialite or Ivy League princess know-it-all. I like her. Holland comes from a very normal background, and for what my opinion is worth, I think she's good for you."

He winked at Nan. "Once again, we agree. I've… enjoyed my time with Holland."

His grandmother's thin eyebrows rose high on her forehead.

"Oh? Dare I hope your time together leads to more between you?"

Max rose from the chair and bussed a kiss across his grandmother's forehead. "It's been less than a week, Nan."

She grasped his hand and held him in position. "If it's right, you know it, Max. Just like I knew it was love with Aki. It happens like that sometimes."

He didn't want to argue with his grandmother when he was getting ready to leave, so he changed the subject to the news of his sister's pregnancy, his mother's latest diet, and then went on to his plans to help Uncle Jack build a school for girls.

"Am I interrupting?"

Max got to his feet and turned, sucking in a breath at Holland's beauty. She wore black leggings and short boots, a silky-looking top, and her leather jacket. Like always she looked casual but dressy enough for pretty much anywhere he might take her to. "You look beautiful."

"Thank you."

He felt the sweep of her brown gaze on him as she took in his jeans and Henley, and wondered if she felt the same singe of heat as he did when he looked at her. "Ready?"

"Yes. Violet, I hope you have a pleasant evening."

"Likewise, dear. You and Max have fun. Oh, Holland? Have you had any luck finding Aki?"

Max was in the process of crossing the room toward Holland and saw how she quickly glanced at him, visibly uncomfortable.

"Um, not yet, Violet, no. But I am looking."

"I know you are, dear. Thank you."

"You're welcome."

Max gently grasped her elbow and leaned in to kiss her on the cheek. "Ready for your surprise?" Maybe it was rude not to acknowledge the exchange that just took place, but he didn't want to start their evening off on a sour note.

"I do like surprises."

He chuckled at her grin and steered her toward the stairs.

"Are you going to tell me where we're going?"

"You'll see," he said, escorting her to the passenger side of his SUV. Once in, he closed the door and sent a text to his contact, alerting them that they were on their way.

Holland chatted about a conversation she'd had with one of her sisters, and he asked a few more questions about the company she worked for and the process of listing his grandmother's things. They approached their destination and he glanced at Holland before making an abrupt right into the park.

"What? Seriously?"

He chuckled at her expression and drove up to the gate of the now closed go-kart track. "Ready to let loose of that speed you're trying to bottle up?"

"Yes, but… it's closed."

"For us. You."

She blinked at the statement, her lips parting and tempting him beyond his restraint. He leaned across the console and stole a quick kiss, lingering once he tasted her.

"I can't believe you did this. Max…"

She grabbed hold of his shirt and pulled him back, kissing him hard and fast and with enough enthusiasm to make him want to stay in the vehicle to see what came next. When they came up for air, they both breathed heavily. "Come on. I want to see you in action."

"HE DID WHAT?"

"You heard me," Holland said on the phone to Ireland. "We had the entire course to ourselves. It was amazing."

"You know," Ireland said, "you're more like Frankie than you want to admit."

Holland chuckled and held the cell phone away while quickly hitting the speaker button, settling into bed with her laptop.

"So how did the night end? That's what I want to know."

Holland blushed when she thought of the hot and heavy make-out session that had taken place in the SUV, one that had singed her skin and practically melted her very bones. "We, um, ran through a drive-thru for dinner."

"Holl?"

"There may have been some kissing." She touched her laptop mouse to awaken the screen and keyed in her password.

"What are you doing? I thought you didn't work after hours?"

"I'm not. This is… personal."

"Oh?"

"Yeah, I'm doing some research for a friend." She found the page she'd bookmarked the last time she'd searched for information on Akihiro Tadashi and started scanning, loving the fact she'd gotten fairly good at multi-tasking over the years.

"Okay, so you and Max."

Holland sighed, wanting to talk about Max so much but unwilling to expose their private moments just yet. "No. I don't want to talk about it."

"You're no fun."

"I beg to differ. I'm loads of fun. You should've seen me on that track. Ireland, it was such a blast."

"Oh, Dominic just walked in. I have to go have some fun with my husband."

"I'm going to hold you to that," Dominic said in the background.

Holland smiled, happy that her sister had found love again. "Get to it, girl. I have some stuff I need to do before bed, too."

"Does this have anything to do with Max? Are you digging into his past?"

"No. Stop worrying."

"Can't. Love you, sister."

"Love you, too. Behave yourself."

"Never. Night." Holland tapped the button to end the call and focused once more on the screen in front of her. Every listing required a bit of reading to suss out whether the man was the right age, if there was a professional biography somewhere listing his history, and—

Holland sucked in a sharp breath and nearly choked on the air.

Right age. And his professional biography said, *Are you him?* Chills ran over her, through her entire body. She quickly saved the page and began a new search based on the information. In short order, she had gathered a huge amount of information, but as badly as she wanted to run shouting the news, she knew she had to be cautious.

And even though it was late, going on ten, should she?

She clicked on the page that listed contact numbers associated with Aki and said a quick prayer as she picked up her phone.

MAX HEARD a soft knock and froze in the act of removing his watch. He'd left Holland at her door earlier with a good-night kiss that made it clear he would welcome more, and now his body tensed at the thought of her standing on the other side.

He tossed the watch atop the dresser and crossed the room with minimal steps, yanking the door open so fast he startled Holland into taking a step back.

She looked adorable. No makeup. Hair pulled haphazardly atop her head in a messy bun. She wore a tank top fitted to her beautiful torso and sleep shorts that... "Turtles?"

"What? Oh," she said. "Um, yeah. I have a thing for turtles. Guess that's another of my secrets. Did I wake you?"

He wore his jeans but had removed his shirt a few minutes before in preparation of stripping down to sleep. "No. I wound up having to deal with some business, so I've been on the phone for the last couple of hours. It's late, though." For the first time, he noticed she carried her laptop and her expression was one of wariness. "Do you want to come in?"

She inhaled and Max had to remind himself to keep his gaze trained on her face.

"N-no. I think... Um, let's go over here."

"Holland, what's going on?"

She backed up a step, two, and then turned, walking barefoot toward the third-floor sitting area that faced the floor-to-ceiling windows.

His gaze lowered, taking in the sway of her hips in those short little turtle shorts, and he knew he'd never see another one and not think of her.

Holland seated herself on the couch and lifted the laptop lid, tapping the keys. Max watched her, an uneasy feeling settling deep. "Holland, what's going on?"

"I... found him."

Dread filled him and he bit back a rare curse. "Akihiro?"

"Yes."

He ran his hand over his face roughly in the struggle to temper his anger. "I wish you would've left that alone."

"I know. But I didn't."

"So what did you find? Did Nan's father lie about his death?"

"Yes."

"Not surprising."

She looked up at him, her expression one of apprehension he guessed was due to his tone. "If you knew my family, you'd understand why I'm not surprised," he told her. "But more than that, he was a father of a teenage daughter in a time when, like it or not, he knew my grandmother would be ostracized alongside Akihiro. Can you blame him for wanting to protect her?"

"It doesn't matter now. All that matters is that I found him and I called and—"

"You mean he's still *alive*?"

She nodded again. "Alive and seemingly well. I-I didn't talk to him. I spoke with his granddaughter. She confirmed that he was in an internment camp in California, and he's a retired botanist."

"Where?"

"Virginia."

Max turned and moved to the window, staring out at the moon over the water. "Don't tell her."

"What? Max, I have to. I promised her I would look and—"

"She doesn't need to know you found him."

"Why not? What are you so afraid of?"

"I'm just trying to protect her, Holland. I insist you

keep this to yourself," he said, turning to face her once more.

Holland lifted her chin and slowly closed the lid of the laptop, holding it against her side as she stood. She barely reached his shoulder in her bare feet, and without the makeup and the clothes and the hair, she appeared younger, more vulnerable. Until he met her gaze and saw the steely strength looking back at him.

"I'm sorry you feel that way because I'm telling her tomorrow."

"Holland—"

He broke off, unsure of what he could possibly say, if anything, to change her mind.

She paused and turned to face him again.

"I don't know why things ended with your ex-fiancée. You've never shared that with me. But I do know this— If I ever loved someone as much as Akihiro and Violet expressed in those letters, and that love was returned in the same measure, I'd move mountains to keep it. Protect it. I didn't share that with David, and you obviously didn't share that with your ex, but your grandmother has a chance to *have that*, Max. How can you stand there and so coldly order me to deny her that blessing?"

Chapter 10

The following morning, Holland dragged herself from bed after a sleepless night, wondering if Max would be gone.

He'd concluded his business days ago, and now that she had refused to abide by his order not to tell Violet the news, well… time would tell.

She quickly showered and dressed, noting that makeup did nothing to hide the shadows beneath her eyes, nor the puffiness that remained from the tears she'd shed out of frustration.

Finally. Finally she'd met a man who interested her on every freaking level only to discover he was afraid of love? Maybe it wasn't the entire truth, but that's certainly what it'd felt like in the dark of night as she hugged her pillow.

She grabbed her laptop and phone and quietly left her room. She was halfway down the stairs when she heard Max's footsteps behind her.

"Holland, please. Don't do this."

"If you could give me a legitimate reason why I shouldn't, I'd consider what you said. But you can't."

She hurried the rest of the way down and entered the

room where Violet sat at the breakfast table.

Up until last night, she'd been wined and dined the world over but she'd never felt the way Max made her feel.

Was she a unicorn? The only woman on earth who hadn't experienced that level of excitement? Attraction? That intrinsic something that stated loud and clear that what she'd had with Max was different?

Was being the key word?

"Good morning, Holland. Max."

"Good morning, Nan."

"Holland, dear, are you all right? Are you not feeling well?"

Holland felt Max's gaze on her, willing her to do his bidding, but she stiffened her spine and squared her shoulders and marched to the table. "I found him, Violet. Aki is alive."

"You… you found him? Truly?"

She nodded, blinking hard to clear the haze of tears that appeared when Violet immediately began crying. The poor woman had cried enough this week, first losing her friend and now… Thankfully these tears were happy tears.

The dishes on the tray Sally carried rattled as she hurried to set it on the table before she, too, pulled a tissue from her apron and dabbed at her eyes.

Max muttered something Holland wasn't able to make out as he crossed the room to swipe a cup from the table. He moved to the carafe of coffee and helped himself.

"Where? How is he?"

Holland pulled out a chair and sank down onto the cushion, hoping it would help ease the trembling that had taken root in her limbs as she ignored Max's glare and informed Violet of the details she knew. "He turns ninety-four in a few days, as I'm sure you probably know."

Violet nodded, smiling.

"I talked briefly with his granddaughter. They share his home in Virginia. She said he had a successful career as a botanist."

"He made it back home," Violet murmured softly.

Once again, Holland nodded. "She said he and his father survived their time in the camp, but his father was very weak and unable to travel afterward. He was free a year before he passed away, and then Akihiro worked his way back across the country. When he got to Virginia, he learned of your marriage.

"He married at some point, had a family. His wife passed many years ago, though, and his granddaughter said he never remarried. I-I have his contact information." She pulled the Post-it Note off of her laptop and left it on the table.

Violet didn't speak and Holland wasn't sure what to do. Sally took a shuddering breath and quietly began removing breakfast from the tray but left the coverings to keep the plates warm.

After a long moment, Violet got to her feet and retrieved her cane from the arm of the chair where it hung. She picked up the note, staring down at it.

"Holland, dear. Thank you. I-I suspected my father lied to me about Aki's death."

"Of course."

"I'm going to go lie down, my dear. I hope you understand."

"Yes, but… is there anything I can do?"

"No. I just need some quiet time to think and pray."

Holland watched as Sally took hold of Violet's arm and slowly helped her employer and friend down the hall toward her suite. Max remained at the windows drinking his coffee, but when she quietly said his name, he turned on his heel and stalked out without a word to her.

Holland sat there a long while before gathering her things and heading for her room. She wrote out a note to Violet explaining that she had all of the photos and information she needed. She thanked her for her hospitality, hoped she hadn't caused her any pain, and packed her suitcase.

Crash and burn, she texted to Ireland once she was in her car.

Several seconds passed before the three little dots appeared.

911 at the dream catcher?

Yeah. Gimme an hour though.

Drive safe.

Holland pulled into her house forty minutes later due to traffic and left her suitcase in the trunk. She entered the empty house and quickly changed into a bathing suit, topping it with shorts and a tank before grabbing a towel as she headed right back out the door. It was a gorgeous day. Plenty warm enough to sit on the sand and take in some rays while she complained about her love life.

She made her way to the dream catcher mailbox a few blocks away, located down on the sand between the ocean and the dunes. Ireland was already there when Holland arrived. "That was fast."

"I've been worried about you. Are you okay?"

"Yeah. Just needing some sister time." She plopped down beside Ireland and linked their arms before laying her head on Ireland's shoulder.

"You realize I'm not buying the stoic face, right?"

She squeezed her sister's arm and stayed quiet, staring at the water and letting the sun and the sand and the surf heal what they could.

Frankie arrived with London from the direction of the pier.

"Carolina's trying to find someone to cover for her at the pier house," Frankie said. "But she's on her way."

"Oh, that's right. I forgot," Ireland murmured. "Baby brain," she said by way of explanation.

Frankie reached over and placed her hand on the growing mound of Ireland's belly.

"Hear that, kid? Your mama is accusing of you being a brain-sucking monster."

"Frankie."

They all laughed at the teasing and Ireland's playful slap in Frankie's direction.

"So what's up?" London asked. "Is something wrong? Ireland, it came from you. Everything okay?"

"She did it for me," Holland said. "I've just missed you guys."

"I take it you're done with the assignment you were on?"

"The in-house stuff, yeah. I have a few finishing touches left to write but I can do that from home."

"Cool," Frankie said. "What's next?"

"Time off, remember?"

"Hey, she made it," Frankie said, lifting her chin to where Carolina jogged toward them.

Caro dropped to her knees on the towel before sliding onto her butt.

"What's up with the Bat signal?"

Ireland nudged Holland. "Go on. Tell them about Max," Ireland said.

Holland lifted her head from Ireland's shoulder so she could glare at her sister. "Really?"

"Who's Max?" London asked.

"And why are you sending hate glares at Ireland? Who is this guy?" Frankie demanded.

"Maximilian Bane," Ireland said.

"The *billionaire?*" Carolina asked, gasping as she got back on her knees in her excitement. *"Seriously?"*

Holland took a deep breath, glared at Ireland, and nodded. "Yes. But… I'm pretty sure it's over."

"Holl, stop being so vague and tell us what happened already," London ordered.

"Wow. You have certainly perfected that mom voice in a short amount of time," Frankie said to her twin, referring to the two adorable twins that would become London's once she and Cooper married.

"Holl. Seriously," London said.

"Yeah, you're stalling and we're not liking it," Frankie added. "You're not you and we can tell. What happened? And how long have you known this guy?"

"Not long."

"Long enough," Ireland corrected. "When it's made you this sad."

"I'm not sure what I am. I mean, yeah, I'm…" Her throat thickened with tears she refused to shed, and it took her a moment to gather herself. "I'm *hurt*. He's angry. It's just not a good situation."

"So did you break up?" Carolina asked. "And can I just freak out for a moment because my sister is or was dating *Maximilian Bane?*"

Frankie shoved Carolina over on the towel and Holland looked at Ireland. "Now do you know why I didn't want to talk about dating him?"

Frankie and London both told Carolina to hush while Ireland hugged Holland close.

"What now? Where did things stand when you last talked?"

Her phone chimed and then began to ring. Holland ignored it and it stopped, but seconds later it began ringing again.

She pulled the phone from the towel and flipped it over to see the screen. Max? She quickly swiped to answer. "Hello?"

"Please tell me you're with her," Max said, his tone urgent and tight.

"What? With who?"

"Nan. She and Sally are both gone."

"Maybe they just went out for some air," Holland said, aware that her sisters listened to every word. "Sally might be trying to cheer Violet up? Get her out of the house?"

"Hang on."

Holland frowned and ignored Ireland's concerned stare. She sat close enough to possibly hear both sides of the conversation, but thankfully, if Ireland could hear, she wasn't sharing.

"I just checked and Nan requested the Bane jet be fueled and waiting for her so she can go visit a friend in Virginia. Thankfully the jet was in Florida, so it bought me some time, but I have get to her before they take off."

"I'll meet you at the airport."

"Holland—"

"Don't you dare tell me not to come," she said, scrambling to her feet.

"Meet me at the house. It's closer," Max said before the phone went dead.

"My bike is parked at the beach access," Frankie said. "I'll take you home."

"Quick, put my jeans on. You can't go like that," London said, looking around at the empty beach before shedding down to her underwear.

Holland quickly gave London the shorts she'd pulled on over her swimsuit and they both wriggled into the denim.

"You can have my top," Carolina said. "It'll look good

over your tank."

Holland yanked the shirt on and followed Frankie to the closest beach access and climbed on.

It took only a few minutes to get back to the house but every one of them felt like an hour. She had to run into the house to grab her purse and keys, but she was right back down the stairs and into her car.

She raced down Dow and prayed the entire time that God would give her a pass and not let her get pulled over. She made it to Carolina Beach Road in record time, a steady stream of prayers in her head as she focused on getting to Violet's as quickly as possible.

It took too long, but considering she'd nearly doubled the speed limit a couple of times getting there, she couldn't complain. She wheeled the car into the drive, where Max waited, and he waved her into the SUV. Not what she wanted to do when her adrenaline was pumping from the wild drive but fine.

Neither of them spoke as Max gunned the gas and got them moving. Finally he looked over to where she sat in the passenger seat and then did a double take.

"What are you wearing?"

She winced at the fact he'd noticed she wasn't her usual put-together self and shrugged. "I was at the beach with my sisters," she said. "These are London's pants, Caro's shirt. But I'm here. Have you talked to Violet or Sally?"

For a short second, his gaze warmed when she'd mentioned her clothing, but just as quickly the warmth faded.

"You look beautiful. And, no. Neither of them will pick up."

They hit traffic along the way because of an accident and Max impatiently squirmed in the driver's seat. Long minutes passed with the tension growing between them.

"I can't believe she's doing this," he muttered.

"I can't believe you can't believe it."

Max glared at her from across the interior.

"Max, he was her first love. Of course she's going to want to see him. I think it's sweet."

"You would. You're a romantic."

"And you like to pretend you're not but you are."

"Come again?"

She nodded repeatedly but kept her gaze on the inching traffic ahead of them. "You are. You want to protect her and that's a hero's heart. And what makes a hero vulnerable? Love. You love her, you're afraid she'll get hurt like you did when things with what's-her-face didn't work out, and now you're afraid to try again, so why should your ninety-four-year-old grandmother try? Am I right?"

"You don't know what happened with me."

"So why don't you tell me."

He hit the steering wheel when the traffic stalled again.

"She wanted my money, didn't mind it that I traveled a lot, and I came home one day to find her in bed with her Pilates instructor."

"You chose wrong. It happens to the best of us," Holland said. "David probably felt the same way about me when I turned him down."

"Did you sleep with your Pilates instructor?"

"Hurt is hurt, Max," she said, ignoring the question. "Let Violet remember the past. Let her see him. Meet him again after all of these years. Just let her enjoy the time she has left here to enjoy. Is that such a bad thing?"

"He could keel over and die tomorrow."

"So could we."

A rough chuckle left Max's chest.

"I'm not going to win with you, am I?"

"I don't know. Do you really want to?"

"You left without saying goodbye."

"I didn't think you'd care."

"I do. But this whole thing with Nan…" He inhaled and exhaled roughly. "I guess this means we've had our first fight."

"I guess it does."

So where did they go from here? Could they survive the world and the drama and the chaos of life in the twenty-first century? "Holland, I have to leave soon. Go back to the village where my uncle and aunt live with the items they desperately need."

He glanced across the expanse and saw her close her eyes and nod.

"I know. I'll be traveling soon, too. Once I take some time off for my sister's baby shower and London's wedding and the like."

Silence descended, the impact of that future distance weighing heavily on them both.

His grandmother had already boarded by the time they made it to the airfield, but Max had ordered the pilot to delay takeoff. Holland heard Violet's gasp when Max entered the plane and quickly moved through the interior to where she sat.

"You've given me a few gray hairs today, Nan."

"I'm going. Please, don't try to stop me, Max. I have to do this."

Max turned so that his grandmother could see Holland standing behind him, and he held up his hand for her to take, motioning Holland to take one of the two seats across from Violet and Sally.

"I know. That's why we're here. I think we all want to meet the man you love."

Chapter 11

Max found his grandmother utterly adorable as she fussed with her hair and makeup during the car ride to Akihiro Tadashi's home. He glanced at Holland and found her watching Nan as well. She must have sensed his attention because her gaze shifted to his. "Thank you."

"For what?" she asked.

"If it wasn't for you, I would've missed this. I love seeing her this way," he whispered. "She's like a schoolgirl."

Holland's smile warmed his heart and did a number on his insides.

"That's why this is so special. Love is precious. It shouldn't be dismissed."

He was finally seeing that. No matter the age.

The driver turned the luxury SUV into a driveway outside of a two-story house, and Max noted the beautiful flowers and landscaping. The man had an eye, that was for sure.

When he'd left the house this morning so angry, he'd made some calls and done a bit of research on Tadashi. By all accounts, he was the honest, hardworking man his grandmother had proclaimed him to be.

The group of them exited the vehicle, and Max welcomed his grandmother's arm through his as they made their way toward the door. He knocked and, after a moment, it opened. The elderly man was dressed in khakis and a crisp white shirt, and his face lit up like a Christmas tree when he recognized who stood on his porch.

"My flower?" the man asked, his voice breaking on the words.

His grandmother burst into tears and laughter and surged forward on her cane, unable to get in the door fast enough.

"Aki. Oh, Aki, I can't believe… I thought you were dead. Oh, *Aki*!"

The two hugged and patted, talking incoherently with tears streaming down their faces.

"Please, come in," a young woman stated from behind them.

She held a baby on her hip, her smile sweet and welcoming.

"I'm Tia, his granddaughter. And this is Mae," she said of the baby.

Max quickly made the introductions while his grandmother and Akihiro continued to stand there and hold each other tight.

Finally the two separated and Max watched as Akihiro produced a handkerchief, giving it to Nan so she could dry her eyes.

"Oh, Aki. I've dreamed of this day. Of seeing you again. I'm so happy."

"I am stunned. What are you doing here?"

Nan explained about her father's lie and how Holland had searched for him.

"I'm sorry we've just shown up like this but I couldn't wait to see you. Not another moment. I had to come."

"I'm glad you didn't wait."

"Aki, did you ever think of me? Of us?"

Max looked around and realized he was the only one not shedding tears. It wasn't from lack of emotion, though. The fist in his chest squeezed tighter and tighter as he listened to their conversation.

"Come," Akihiro said. "Follow me. Please."

Akihiro took Nan's hand and, side by side, they walked to the back of the house. Tia hitched the baby higher on her hip and motioned for them to follow.

"You'll want to see," Tia said. "I've always wondered who she was. Such a gift to finally know."

Sally went first, with Holland and Max following. Tia and the baby brought up the rear as they all exited the house onto a beautifully designed brick patio and Japanese garden. A path led the way to a large atrium, and once there, Akihiro swung open double doors.

"Did I think of you? Every day of my life," the man said.

"Oh, my word. Max, look at the violets," Holland said. "There are *hundreds and hundreds* of them."

Max swallowed hard. If ever there was proof the man loved his grandmother…

"Oh, Aki. Oh, they're so beautiful," Nan said, crying again.

"Never as beautiful as you," the man said. "I had a good life, as did you, but I never forgot my flower. Nor did I stop loving her."

Holland held a hand to her face, her expression one of pure awe and heartfelt love and silent tears. Max wrapped his arm around her shoulders and tucked her to his side, deciding then and there, as she pressed her face against his chest and held tight, that she would get the same kind of love and devotion for the next seventy-nine years if she would have him. "Holland, we can let jobs and distance separate us." He kissed the top of her head and used his free hand to lift her chin to better see her face. "Or we can commit to doing whatever it takes to see where this could go. Maybe it's too soon to declare our love, but after knowing you little more than a week, I do know I feel more than I have for any woman," he said, thanking God he'd seen the ex-fiancée for what she was before it was too late. Otherwise he wouldn't be here now. "Like you once told me, love means something and it's worth fighting for, and I'd very much like to learn what we could be. If it's something like this," he said, tilting his head toward the atrium. "What do you say?"

She nodded rapidly, her voice thick when she said, "This. I want *this.*"

Max pulled her close and kissed her, not stopping until she made that little sound that called to him, told him that whatever love they'd lost in the past had been found in each other. "Me, too, sweetheart. Me, too," he said against her lips, adding, "And maybe during your time off, I can sweep you off to Africa."

Epilogue

Six months later…

Holland stared out at the waterway and sighed, wondering how it was possible to feel so content. She and Max had spent a lot of time physically apart in the last six months but they'd talked or video-chatted every one of those days. He'd even whisked her off to Africa and shown her the area and the people he loved so much. She'd met his aunt and uncle, and watched Max in action. Talk about a sight to behold. Seeing him surrounded by all of the village children, laughing and playing… Just when she thought she couldn't love him more, she found her heart expanding.

"Hey, you."

Holland smiled when Max's strong arms slid around her waist and she felt his lips on her neck.

"There you are."

"Miss me?" she asked.

"Always. Enjoying the view?"

"Mmm. I love it that everyone is here and getting along. Well, for the most part," she said, thinking of the political debate she'd left inside between her father and his. "How are the fathers doing? Come to blows yet?"

"They're fine. Everyone's making their way outside."

Max had suggested hosting a family dinner so that everyone could meet each other and Violet had loved the idea so much it had turned into quite the party. Aki's family had arrived yesterday, and Holland's entire family and the Banes had been showing up for the last several hours. Her sisters had shown up in force, all smiles and laughter and gasps as Holland had shown them around Violet's beautiful home.

Max loosened his hold, and she mourned the loss of his touch when he withdrew from her.

"Holland."

Holland turned to find everyone standing outside along the beautiful patio facing her. Her sisters' husbands held cameras or phones pointed in her direction while the girls had champagne glasses held at the ready. Except for Ireland who held baby Isaleigh and bounced the chubby baby in her arms. "What's happening? Did I miss something?" she asked, searching the crowd for Violet and Aki. The two lovebirds were seated on a couch, holding hands as well as champagne glasses.

Max grinned and lowered himself to one knee, producing an exquisite ring. Holland gasped, her eyes stinging with tears when she realized Violet wasn't the one getting a proposal.

"Holland Cohen, I love you. And I want to spend the rest of my life with you. Will you marry me?"

She nodded, unable to speak due to the lump in her throat, and held out her shaking hand. Max placed the gorgeous cushion cut diamond on her finger and straightened, using his hold on her fingers to tug her toward him while the group cheered and toasted them. Holland dove into his arms and lifted her face to his for a kiss that took her breath and gave her life at the same time. She'd waited so long for this. This man, this feeling. The lost kind of love she'd always hoped to find but feared no longer existed.

It did exist. The man in her arms was proof.

WANT TO CONTINUE READING KAY'S WORK? BELOW IS AN EXCERPT OF HEALING HER COWBOY, **THE FIRST NOVEL IN KAY'S MONTANA SECRETS SERIES.**

EXERPT FROM HEALING HER COWBOY:

GRACE KORBIT FLINCHED when a book slammed against the wall three feet to the right of her head.

"Next time I won't miss. Get out."

Gathering her courage, she peered into Seth Rowland's bedroom, unable to see much because of the dark blinds covering the windows. Too bad they didn't block the smell. Musty air and a decidedly unpleasant aroma assailed her.

"You gotta hearing problem? None of you've managed to fix me yet and I'm sick of waiting for a miracle."

Grace was shocked. This wasn't the Seth she remembered. Taking a deep breath, she ignored his order and went inside, hoping her instincts would protect her from any additional flying objects. Three steps in, her foot landed on something soft and skidded an inch to the left. *Eeeew.*

But the goo sticking to her foot explained the smell. At least part of it. The pungent odor of a too-ripe banana filled her nostrils. She lifted her shoe, hobbling momentarily and, using the light streaming in from the connecting bedroom, spotted the outline of an overflowing trash can. She shook her foot over the container until she heard a dull *thunk.*

"How about I open the blinds and windows?" she asked, her voice husky as she scraped the sole of her shoe over the edge. That done, a steadying breath full of dust and the lingering smell of fruit propelled her quickly through the mess.

"How about you go—" Seth finished his crude suggestion. Grace winced, but she'd heard worse.

She trailed her fingers along the wall until they found the drawstring pull of the blind and yanked hard, although she regretted it instantly when the dust flew. She waved one hand in front of her face while unlocking the sash with the other. Cold, crisp air flowed in.

Seth's eyes bored a hole into her back as Grace made her way to the second window, thankful the sunlight enabled her to maneuver around the messy room, which looked as though it hadn't been cleaned in weeks.

Mindful of the dust, she raised this blind slower, giving the task more attention than it deserved due to a sudden nervousness. How had she ever convinced herself she could do this? See Seth again? Talk to him, *touch* him? But in the same vein, how could she have said no?

She stared outside, at the dirt-and-gravel road leading away from the house, and knew this was one window she'd better keep closed. Otherwise she'd have a hard time fighting the temptation to climb through and make a run for it.

Unable to postpone the inevitable any longer, she turned. "Seth, I—" Grace gasped at the sight of him and hated herself because she wasn't quick enough to squelch the revealing sound. He heard, too, because his gaze narrowed on her and she knew the exact moment he recognized her—and she realized in an instant Jake hadn't told Seth his ex-girlfriend was to be his next physical therapist.

Seth's eyes widened, then he looked away. But in that moment in between she saw it all. Saw the cold, bitter distance she'd created. The anger and upset and breath-stealing pain.

Seth's guarded stare reminded her of an injured, cornered animal, fighting back out of instinct, but unsure of whether or not he really wanted to continue the battle.

Oh, Seth.

Lucky for her he appeared as shocked to see her as she was to see him in such a condition. She fell back on six years of training and experience. Lessons hard learned and refined by taking on some of the most difficult cases others had given up on. Like Seth.

Squaring her shoulders, she swallowed. "It's good to see you, Seth. Do you throw books at everyone who comes through the door or just me?"

Jaw tight, he continued to glare. "I thought you were—Ah, hell *no*," he growled as understanding replaced his shock.

She forced herself to move closer with a confidence she didn't feel. "That's right. I'm your new therapist."

Grace crossed her arms over her chest, hoping it looked like a gesture of strength, even arrogance, instead of what it really was—an attempt to control her quivering limbs.

He laughed, the sound gruff and low, sending shivers through her.

Seth glowered at the door. "Jake!"

Moving forward another step, she was amazed at the difference in the man she'd known compared to the one before her. Ten years ago Seth had been clean-cut and entirely too handsome, God-gifted with one of those rugged, craggy faces that only got better with age. Tall and lanky, he'd had a natural swagger and smile that stopped what little traffic North Star, Montana, could lay claim to.

Now the handsome cowboy was gone, and in his place was a bitter and broken man with eyes that burned hot with anger, and an appearance that stated quite clearly Seth didn't care what happened to him. Not anymore.

"He isn't——"

"*Jake!*" When Jake didn't appear, Seth turned to her. "You've had your look at the cripple, now get out."

Her nails dug into the flesh of her arms. The sharp pain stiffened her resolve and reminded her, for the moment at least, she was the one in charge. She just had to prove it to Seth. And to herself.

"I can't leave you like this."

He laughed without humor. "You didn't have a problem leaving me before. Now's no different."

Now *was* different, but her reasoning was the same. And as badly as she wanted to do as he said, to turn tail and run, she was just as determined to stay.

She shook her head. "I'm good at what I do, Seth. What do you say? Will you work with me?"

A vicious curse filled the air, succinct with fury.

"Fine, I'll leave," she said, careful to keep her voice from shaking even as she raised it to be heard over his ongoing litany. Seth stilled, then smirked in triumph, and that's when she decided he needed a firm kick in the rear. "That is, when you're able to get out of that bed and throw me out yourself."

Neither of them moved. They wound up playing a childish game of Stare Down until finally, Seth bit out yet another long string of curses. "Jake had no right!"

"He's desperate to help you."

Help him? Seth scowled at her. There was no helping him. With every day that passed and every therapist that came and went, the angrier he became, because nothing happened. Nothing. The doctors' diagnoses were wrong.

"You can't." He jerked his head toward the door. "Don't let it hit you on the way out. Better yet, do."

Dust mites floated through the air as she stood there wearing an expression so pitying he wanted to hurl something at her again.

Tall and athletic, Grace still had a natural beauty. Her strength showed in the way her shoulders were squared and braced. The way her chin jutted in determination.

He'd kissed that chin. Run his hands over her body and listened as she sighed, loving the sound and loving her despite the way she'd immediately pull away and establish distance between them. He should've realized she didn't feel the same about him, should've known something was wrong before he'd made a fool of himself.

"I understand your anger at being paralyzed, Seth. I'd be angry, too."

He laughed, unable to quell the bitterness. What a line, that. How could she possibly understand? Had she ever had to ask for help to take a leak? Endured the indignity of having an audience present for the sole purpose of making sure he didn't fall off the pot the first time he was able to actually use a toilet instead of a bedpan? *No one* understood.

"You don't understand so don't pretend you do. You want to move and you move. You want to walk and you walk. I *don't*."

"I'm here to help you fix that."

He searched for something else to throw. Not at her, just something to take the edge off. "I don't want you here! You couldn't wait to get out of town ten years ago, but at least you did us both a favor and left before I did something stupid like ask to marry you!"

"I'm sorry," she murmured, her eyes avoiding his. "I should've handled things between us better, but I didn't want to hurt you and I—I wanted to go to college."

"I never would've asked you not to go and you know it. You had a choice, Grace. Two scholarships—a school here where we could've seen each other or a school back east. You made your decision. You left in the middle of the night and ran, as fast and as far as you could, dragging Brent behind you."

"You wouldn't listen to me," she argued. "Things were going too fast. I tried to tell you that—"

He ran a hand over his face. "Any slower and molasses would've beaten us in a race. You made your point. You wanted away from me," he said. "Now I want away from you. You're not welcome here, Grace. Get out of my house, off my ranch and don't come back."

Grace flinched at his words but didn't say anything. Instead of leaving, she approached his hospital bed, making her way through the minefield of books, plastic plates and ranching magazines. Now, there was a kicker. He could read about ranching, but he'd never again be able to do the physical labor he loved so much.

"You have to deal with this," she said, nodding to indicate his legs. "Lying here is getting you nowhere, and I can't leave you like this if for no other reason than what we once meant to each other."

"And what was that?" Seth injected a cruelness into his tone that belied all acknowledgment of their past. He slid his gaze over her again, hoping, praying, she'd go scurrying from the room the way his sister-in-law, Maura, always did. Not Grace though. No, she simply lifted her chin another notch, making him grit his teeth so hard pain shot up to his temple.

He couldn't take his eyes off her, though. Mostly

because he was beginning to notice new things about her. Like how her chest rose and fell with her breathing, how she was too thin for her height and her clothes were baggy, as though the weight loss was recent. Shadows stained the skin beneath her green eyes and she looked tired and drawn. Even a bit brittle. As if a good strong wind would make those board-straight shoulders of hers snap.

Had she worried about coming to Montana and facing him after what she'd done? Heaven above, he couldn't help but think she'd never have had the courage to return had he been healthy and whole and the man he'd once been.

He stared at her chest and the fullness there, not giving a rat's ass if he offended her or made her uncomfortable, as it always had in the past. Problem was instead of intimidating *her*, the sight nearly undid *him*.

"You're fired."

"You can't fire someone you didn't hire."

Her voice was husky and rich, tart, like warm, mulled cider on a fall night.

"I'm staying, Seth, and you'd better get used to having me around. The sooner the better."

She followed her brassy warning with a shrug, but the movement was stiff, and now that she stood within reaching distance, he saw a slight quiver to her hands. The twitch of a muscle near her too full lips. Maybe she *was* nervous about facing him. He hoped so, anyway. God knew he had little else to hope for anymore.

"I will make you a deal, though…if you're interested." She propped her hands on her hips, widened her stance.

He almost laughed at the sight. Almost. Because like it or not, he was curious as to what she was offering.

"What deal?"

"I'll leave…if you can beat me at arm wrestling."

Then he did laugh. "You can do better than that,

Grace," he murmured, relishing the dark flush that stole over her cheeks at his tone.

Her wide, full mouth pursed. "Arm wrestling is a matter of strength. If you can beat me at that, you should be able to handle your wheelchair fairly well. I'll let Jake know, and maybe if you're lucky, he'll back off on wanting you in therapy. Unless you're afraid to lose."

"I wouldn't lose."

"Then what's the problem?"

She meant it. She actually had the nerve to stand there and taunt him. He sucked in a sharp breath as the red-blooded male in him staggered. Grace was strong, no doubt about it, but he was still bigger, broader, with more than thirty years of ranch life under his belt and enough anger to self-combust. "You'll leave?"

"With bells on."

CONTINUE READING HEALING HER COWBOY OR FIND NEW WORKS IN HER LIST. THANK YOU AND HAPPY READING!

MONTANA SECRETS SERIES

- HEALING HER COWBOY
- IT HAD TO BE YOU
- HERS TO KEEP
- MILLION DOLLAR STANDOFF
- HIS CHRISTMAS WISH
- THEIR SECRET SON

Books Also Set in Carolina Cove

CAROLINA COVE SERIES:

- SEASCAPES AND VEGAS MISTAKES
- SEASHELLS AND WEDDING BELLS
- SEA GLASS AND SECOND CHANCES
- SEA BLUE AND LOVING YOU
- SEA VIEW AND SOMETHING NEW

MAKE ME A MATCH SERIES:

- ROMANCE RESET
- RULES OF ENGAGEMENT
- THE MATCHMAKER'S SECRET
- PERFECTLY MISMATCHED
- BY THE BOOK

THE SEASIDE SISTERS SERIES:

- THE LAST GOODBYE

- LATTES AND LULLABYES
- MAP OF DREAMS
- WORTH THE RISK
- LOST LOVE FOUND

BONUS CONTENT:
Excerpt of Seascapes and
Vegas Mistakes

Chapter 1

Hey, I can tell you're exhausted from your week in Vegas but what's up with you?" Amelia asked, sliding Izzy a searching glance from the driver's seat. "I thought you'd be bouncing off the walls with excitement."

Isabel Shipley—Izzy to her friends and family—lifted a hand to rub her upper chest and wondered if it was time to break down and take something for the anxiety plaguing her ever since waking up in her hotel room this morning on her last day in Las Vegas.

The rumpled bed had said a lot of things, but it was the running shower and suddenly pounding head that wouldn't allow her to put two and two together and come up with anything other than sheer panic. Especially when a glance at the bedside clock gave her barely an hour to get to the airport and through Vegas security for her flight back home to Carolina Cove, North Carolina.

Given her frantic state to get out while the gettin' was good, she'd scrambled into clothes she'd purposely left out because she *always* ran late and grabbed the suitcase she had haphazardly packed the day before on a break from the gallery. After a last horrified glance at the open bathroom door and the scrumptiousness she left behind, she'd made a run for the hills and hopefully the return of her sanity.

She didn't *do* things like this. Ever.

So why had she?

Adrenaline had given her just enough mindfulness to hail a taxi, but the TSA line was long and she'd had to freaking *run* for her gate, arriving mere seconds before the door to the plane shut behind her as the last one to board.

Head throbbing from the stress ice pick stabbing her brain, she'd curled up against the window, her mind racing with questions and embarrassment as memories of the previous night surfaced until she fell into a fitful doze that came from too much stress, not enough sleep, a physical soreness that brought a blush to her cheeks.

Hours after leaving the hotel room and Vegas behind, her mind still hadn't come up with any logical answers. Truthfully, she couldn't even blame the champagne she'd drunk.

She'd only had three glasses over a span of time, but her excitement and adrenaline had known no bounds. And what better way to celebrate the completion of her first *real* showcase than with a tall, dark, and very gorgeous man?

He'd made her tingle. Like, seriously, *tingle*. She hadn't known such a thing was possible. Even more amazing, he'd seemed genuinely interested in her art and process, which was *such* a turn-on itself.

He also knew her cousin Michael and had attended her showcase because of it—which made him safer than the average Joe.

"Izzy? Seriously, you're worrying me. What's up?" her best friend asked.

Izzy watched as Amelia ran a hand over her rapidly expanding belly in a soothing-mama gesture and swallowed hard. She had to snap out of it. If anyone should be freaking out, it was Amelia. She was the one with twins on the way.

Izzy nodded to herself. *Suck it up, buttercup.* What was done was done. She and Everett had flirted, sipped luscious champagne, played blackjack and…made a bet. Which was how she'd wound up listening to the shower spray in the next room.

Winner gets a kiss, he'd said.

Loser has to— "I-I…I'm fine. Just really, *really* tired." Because while her challenge hadn't been anything outrageous, it *had* led to the aftermath.

"But your show was a success? You texted and said you'd scored some good commissions and would text me later to tell me details."

Thankful for the distraction, Izzy turned her attention to the passing scenery. "Yeah, sorry about that. I went to the bar for a drink and…talked to friends."

Friend, rather. That's where she'd met him again. The handsome not-so-stranger who'd wandered through the gallery around each of her paintings as though looking over a Monet or something equally amazing. Everett had introduced himself as a longtime friend of her cousin Michael's, said that he'd seen her name on the signs about the gallery show, and remembered Michael bragging about his talented artist cousin and the timing of her upcoming show.

They'd chatted briefly, her entire body humming with excitement because he was so…*so fine.*

But it wasn't until later when she'd met up with him in the bar that things had gone from casual conversation to major flirtation.

"I thought as much. You know, sometimes it really comes down to the people you know, which is why it's so important to get out there. So? Tell me. Who bought your work? Anyone famous?"

Izzy frowned. She'd stayed so busy in Las Vegas prepping for the show after the last-minute inclusion that she hadn't had time to miss home. But now that she was here?

The familiar sights and traffic signs pointing to Carolina Cove brought tears to her eyes and comfort to her soul.

Or maybe it was the relief that she could almost shut herself inside her apartment and pretend the last twelve hours hadn't happened?

Or relive them.

To be honest, it was a toss-up as to which she'd prefer.

How could a thirty-two-year-old woman get herself into such a pickle?

God forbid she ever admit this, but maybe her mother was right? She was too old for this. The games that came with dating and…

It's not dating when it's a one-night stand.

Which she didn't do.

Ever.

Except with someone Michael knows?

Her cousin wasn't a saint by any means, but she was pretty sure he wouldn't want to go to a business meeting and find out what had happened to his "kid cousin" in Vegas. And if memory served, Michael and Everett were currently working on a project.

Great. Oh, great.

"Iz?"

She had to really focus to remember Amelia's question. "Um, I-I don't know. The buyers finalized everything with the curator. I'll get more details this week, I'm sure.

There...wasn't much time there at the end." Because she'd finished the show floating on a cloud, having made plans to meet Everett to celebrate the completion.

"Well, it's fantastic. I'm so proud of you," Amelia said, sliding Izzy another glance from across the way as she crossed the bridge toward Carolina Cove.

"Thanks. I mean, they could always change their mind but—"

"No buts. It's awesome and doubtful that would happen, so accept the sales as a win. I'm happy for you."

"Yeah. It's just...surreal." *In so many ways.*

She appreciated Amelia's support. Her friend was the best, softhearted and understanding and supportive even though Izzy's crazy ideas weren't always thought through.

"Okay, so, you're only minutes away from home. Take today off to recoup and rest, and then you can hit the ground running tomorrow."

"Yeah, I think I might." Sleep was good. It would bring clarity. Right? Maybe then she could figure out exactly how she'd gone from being a not-so-wild child to waking up with a virtual stranger.

She'd had boyfriends. Two long-term ones and a handful of wannabes. But despite what people—especially her mother—might believe about artists and her so-called bohemian lifestyle, she wasn't a casual hookup kind of girl.

And other than talking and laughing and kissing—a *lot* —she wasn't sure when the scales had tipped during the night. Only that she'd allowed Everett to walk her to her hotel room in the wee hours of the morning after all their fun—and then invited him inside.

"Thanks again for picking me up."

"Absolutely. The timing couldn't have worked out better. I can drop you off and head to the film location to look around and still make it home early. I want to do something special for Lincoln's birthday. Especially since this is our last birthday alone for a while."

Izzy watched as Amelia slid her hand over her pregnant belly again and loved how happy her friend seemed to be. Pregnancy definitely agreed with her. "Good thing I have my sunglasses on," she teased. "You're absolutely glowing."

Amelia laughed, her earrings brushing her shoulders as she shrugged.

"I feel like it. I mean, it's weird but I have all of this *energy*. I'm told it's not the norm and usually the opposite is true, but I think I could climb mountains with energy to spare."

Izzy thought of how tired her older sister, Allie, had been during her pregnancies and shook her head. Definitely not the norm. "Just don't overdo it," Izzy said, wishing she could borrow some of that energy right now. Maybe then she wouldn't feel as though she'd been dragged out to sea by a riptide and been swimming against the current for days.

"Oh, I won't. I couldn't if I wanted to. Lincoln has been waiting on me hand and foot when I get home from work, and no one on set will let me lift a finger. Oh! Crap."

"What?"

"Well, before I forget...I ran into the Babes while you were gone."

"And?"

"I hate to say it, but your mom *insists* we use her house for the baby shower you're hosting. I hope that's okay? When I told them we were going to have it downstairs at London's Lattes, the Babes...well, they made it *really* hard to say no."

No doubt they had. The Babes rarely took no for an

answer to anything. But why should they when the five older women had been catered to their whole lives?

During the summers of '58 and '59, four prominent Carolina Cove neighbors and friends had given birth to baby girls. One even had a set of twins. The proud mothers had taken the babes for daily strolls in their prams—and the locals had nicknamed them the Boardwalk Babes—a name used to this day by the now sixty-somethings.

All in all, Izzy had four pseudo aunts and ten "cousins," seven female and three male—with the twin Babes each having a set of twins of their own—ranging in age from mid-forties all the way down to Izzy's thirty-two. Growing up, it had sucked to always be the youngest. Even more so because not only had her two older sisters treated her like the baby but all of her "cousins" had as well. She'd always been the kid sister no one wanted tagging along to dampen their fun.

"Okay," Amelia said, turning down the street toward London's Lattes and pulling to a stop behind Izzy's VW Bug convertible. Betty the Bug might be old, but she was still just as pretty as the day Izzy had bought her. Minus a little sun damage the south was known for.

"Need help getting in?" Amelia asked.

"No. I've got it. Thanks."

Izzy had rented the apartment above the coffee shop a little over a year ago when London Cohen, owner of London's Lattes, had met and then married a northern transplant who'd moved to the beach with his adopted children. Making rent wasn't always easy with her sporadic sales, but there was no denying being on her own gave Izzy a sense of freedom and independence she'd longed for after far too many years under her parents' roof.

Living a minimalist lifestyle made it easier to live sale to sale, but it didn't leave much in the bank afterwards. Not that her parents needed to know that. But thankfully with her commissions from the Vegas showcase, she now had a cushion that would allow her to breathe for at least six months. She would put that time to good use.

Her mother had never understood why Izzy felt the need to move out of their garage apartment into an apartment several blocks away, but Izzy knew if she ever had a hope of proving her abilities and worth, she had to stand on her own. Even if it meant giving up more than a few luxuries. Life was about more than just things. It was experiences and moments…moments she captured and painted because she couldn't imagine doing anything else with her life—no matter what her family said.

"Okay, so get in there and get some rest. You don't seem like yourself, and you'll need all the energy you can muster now that the Babes are involved in the baby shower. I have a feeling things might be a little over-the-top now."

"Ain't that the truth," Izzy muttered, pulling her lips into a wry twist of dread. If her mother and the rest of the Babes knew one thing, it was how to entertain. Nothing could be simple. A party—especially a baby shower welcoming a new life into the world—would be "Babe-ified" in the extreme.

"Sorry. I know I should've protested more, but you know how they can be."

"Trust me, I know," Izzy said truthfully. "And it's not a problem. I'm used to dealing with my mother and the Babes. No worries." While navigating the Babes might make shower prepping more stressful, Izzy wouldn't be responsible for footing the bill on the Babes' many additions to the planning. If nothing else, that was a win for her in a time when she needed to bank and save as much as she could for a rainy day.

"Iz?"

Izzy was halfway out the door when Amelia stopped her. "Yeah?"

"What's with the ring? You're pretty eclectic but that's not exactly your usual style," Amelia said with a wry expression and a little laugh.

Izzy glanced down at the gaudy, sparkling double dice ring she wore on the ring finger of her left hand. One she'd thought about taking off on the plane but hadn't because of the memories it now held in the somewhat sensual-coated space in her brain from last night.

The fun of three glasses of bubbly seemed like a good idea while she had such a great time with a handsome, charismatic man. "Oh, it's just, um, a souvenir," she said, swallowing hard because of the way her heart began to pound in her chest when an image appeared in her mind. The champagne-coated edges of her memories sharpened, and she zeroed in on the moment her gorgeous companion had slid the ring onto her finger, a smile on his seductive lips that she'd matched with one of her own.

"Good thing. For a second there I thought you'd gone and gotten married in Vegas."

Izzy released a laugh that sounded shriller than she'd intended and slid her purse to her shoulder. "You know how it goes. What happens in Vegas stays in Vegas."

Also by Kay Lyons

MONTANA SECRETS SERIES:

- HEALING HER COWBOY
- IT HAD TO BE YOU
- HERS TO KEEP
- MILLION DOLLAR STANDOFF
- HIS CHRISTMAS WISH
- THEIR SECRET SON

THE SEASIDE SISTERS SERIES:

- THE LAST GOODBYE
- LATTES AND LULLABYES
- MAP OF DREAMS
- WORTH THE RISK
- LOST LOVE FOUND

TAMING THE TULANES SERIES:

- SMALL TOWN SCANDAL
- THEIR SECRET BARGAIN
- CROSSING THE LINE
- THE NANNY'S SECRET
- SOMEONE TO TRUST

THE STONE RIVER SERIES:

- WORTH THE WAIT
- NOT BY SIGHT

- THROUGH THE VALLEY
- LEAD ME NOT
- CHRISTMAS AT HOLLY WOOD
- THEIR CHRISTMAS MIRACLE
- SECOND CHANCES

SMALL TOWN SCANDALS SERIES:

- BRODY'S REDEMPTION
- FALLING FOR HER BOSS
- WITH THIS MAN

SECRET SANTA SERIES:

- SECRET SANTA
- SECRET SANTA II: A CHRISTMAS TO REMEMBER

MAKE ME A MATCH SERIES:

- ROMANCE RESET
- RULES OF ENGAGEMENT
- THE MATCHMAKER'S SECRET
- PERFECTLY MISMATCHED
- BY THE BOOK

CAROLINA COVE SERIES:

- SEASCAPES AND VEGAS MISTAKES
- SEASHELLS AND WEDDING BELLS
- SEA GLASS AND SECOND CHANCES
- SEA BLUE AND LOVING YOU
- SEA VIEW AND SOMETHING NEW

About the Author

Kay Lyons always wanted to be a writer, ever since the age of seven or eight when she copied the pictures out of a Charlie Brown book and rewrote the story because she didn't like the plot. Through the years her stories have changed but one characteristic stayed true— they were all romances. Each and every one of her manuscripts included a love story.

Published in 2005 with Harlequin Enterprises, Kay's first release was a national bestseller. Kay has also been a HOLT Medallion, Book Buyers Best and RITA Award nominee. Look for her most recent novels with Kindred Spirits Publishing.

For more information regarding her work, please visit Kay at the following:

www.kaylyonsauthor.com

@KayLyonsAuthor (Twitter)

Kay Lyons Author (Facebook)

Author_Kay_Lyons (Instagram)

Kay Lyons, Author (Pinterest)

SIGN UP FOR KAY'S NEWSLETTER AND RECEIVE UPDATES ON NEW RELEASES, CONTESTS, PRE-RELEASE BOOK INFORMATION, EXCLUSIVES AND MORE!

www.ingramcontent.com/pod-product-compliance
Lightning Source LLC
Chambersburg PA
CBHW011600190726
48287CB00010B/2992